The Corner of Seduction and Pleasure

Morris Gamble

DEDICATION

In sincere regards and thanks I offer these words to those whom have touched my heart over the years.

CONTENTS

CROSSWALK

PLEASURE

ACKNOWLEDGMENTS

THE MOST HIGH TO WHOM ALL PRAISES ARE WORTHY AND DUE. ASIM BADR AQIL ALI EL, ACHIYAH TEMIMAH SHARIQI-NAHYSSON: AN EVER LEARNING EXPERIENCE OF LOVE AND LIFE.

SEDUCTION

Let Me Write You

It's the Ménage of my pad and pen

It's the fall of an angel in sin

Giving in to corruption

Erotic ways of touching

Your mind with my pen until you're blushing

It's my stroke between lines

The way that your signs

Point to arousal

I'll show you how to

Sit back relax and let pleasure shroud you

In the comfort of my words

The excitement of your verbs

Your passion flowing from my thoughts

The freakish description of all that you've sought

That you mind ventured to but your body knew not

Brought to your reality

It's your pleasure that's having me

Scribble pleasure phrases along your mocha skin

Stroke your excitement from beginning to end

Engraving eroticism into your thoughts until you give in

To the rhythmic feel of my thrusts

Compelling inks orgasm as my pen bursts

Causing the quiver of your sheets

As your honey nectar slowly seeps

But I won't stop until your story is complete

Climax cunningly rises in stages

We move from position to position by turning the pages

Of your fantasies, thoughts and erotic dreams

Stroking from side to side, up to down your fantasy screams

Some mumbled gibberish but I know what it means

Fluent in erotica's language I have the translation

That you wanted to remain lost in sensuality's sensation

Of my deep intense strokes that causes your waters eruption

The caress of your walls that keeps your river gushing

Pounding your ocean's bottom keeping those waves rushing

Beyond lips over and down your thighs

The convulsion of your stomach book marking your sighs

Picking up where we left off more than a trend

Reviewing chapters of orgasm again and again

Until we know the novel of climax beginning to end

Icing on the Cake

Her body was the icing on the cake. It was the depths of her personality and conversation that I thoroughly enjoyed dining on. The way she spoke was divinely eloquent. As words rolled of her tongue and massaged the depths of my soul I became engulfed in her mannerisms. Cordially unpretentious her actions allowed me to relax and just be me. Every conversation we shared left a new impression. The complexity of her essence left an impression that took my thoughts to intrigues paradise. The mellow eased simplicity of our interaction gave the impression of the souls of two lovers reincarnated drawn together by destiny's magnetism.

That sexy lingerie was just icing on the cake. It was merely the decoration of her passions sweetness and her winding curvaceous body which was that of a swirl in marble cake, a triple fudged chocolate delight waiting for my tongue prints to be placed atop its warmth. Her touch is that of the morning's first drop of dew upon the petal of a rose, enticing the full bloom of passion arousing the butterflies of my stomach to confidently fall into the intoxication of her embrace

Our all night love making is more than icing on the cake. Its an erotic adventure shared by two souls walking the same path hand in hand as lover, confidants, friends and eternal companions. The way that our bodies intertwine perfectly is like the conjoining loops of a figure eight resting on its side as our souls chuckle at the thought of a love so infinite. Our relationship from friends to lovers is that of day and night, although only one may be seen at a time the other is always there as co-existing entities completing one another to perfection.

Dream State

She awoke to a position all too familiar to arousal, her sheets drenched from last night's encounter with subliminal desires of she and I engulfed in touching teasing, groping grabbing, clutching pleasing, stroking and stabbing from every position that she enjoyed. The long strokes of my tongue that she once only imagined through the words of my poetry were now the reality of her dreams. It seems I'd touched the depths of her desire. Her desire to feel me deep inside her warmth, deep inside her mental, deep inside her emotional, deep inside her physical state of contradictive pleasures. Contradictingly alone in the night, together with her thoughts of us but there I was so real no longer a figment of her imagination but the reality of a tongue curdling, body numbing, sheet drenching, panty soaking fantasy. More than a dream, some say that dreams are the precursors to our reality foreshadowing what's to come. What's to cum…what is to come between you and I ? A breakfast of you and I, that's what you awoke to an intimate connection between strangers, friends, lovers and companions who shared more than the intimate connection of the physical but also the intimate connection of minds. Two souls strolling the path of life, one three and a half steps behind the other, neither one knowing exactly where this road would lead so they move beyond reason faithfully toward a common goal a common dream and a common light. Both leading the way taking turns carrying the others burdens. How did it come to this? Me being your late night pacification, your late night dreams causing your early mornings shaking simply stated. The reason you wake up ringing out your panties. Damn, I'm jealous of those panties. So close, so near so snug drenched with your essence will you drench me with your essence in the deep blue of midnight? Can I be the star that guides your desires through the night to an early morning resting place of tropical shores, cool breezes, palm trees and white sands? My stroke sensually caressing your sands again and again until you explode into the full screams of my name's crescendo in the words "You know I like it deep." Your body arches closer to mine as our souls ascend to the skies and watch our fleshly desires, rousing a cool gentle breeze that sends chills down your back until they become one as we become one mind, one soul, one heart's beat and one journey shared by two vessels. We become the perfection of Adam and Eve without knowledge of knowledge only the knowledge of knowing one another's companionship through the grace of the most high.

Whole Heartedly

Your lips touch, hips sway, eye contact a beautiful compilation

The way we fit one another without complication

Condensation flowing from eyes signs of elation

Wherever you lead picture me chasing

A dream of refreshing

Touch of God's blessing

Picture us nesting

In an oasis where pleasure awaits us

Chocolate delight drools at the chance to taste us

My heart pounds out a rhythm of Anxious

But the tone of your voice reassures me with "Patience"

That good things come to those who wait

More than coincidence and chance its fate

Forever and eternal won't you be my mate

As our souls dance no need to contemplate

How I love you…whole heartedly

Want to be with you and only you… whole heartedly

Desire to spend the rest of my life with you …whole heartedly

Have faith in our love…whole heartedly

10 seconds in love's Vacuum

We stand fingertips interlocked beyond metacarpals, toe to toe, face to face. No words being exchanged, silently gazing into one another's soul amidst a whirlwind of communication. Energy conducted from the rapid pounding of our hearts which cause jugulars pulse to knock at the door of eruption. Palms forecast of humidity expresses the anxiety that we both share. Ohms of giddiness vibrate through arms, race up shoulder and cascade down opposite arm until it transmits our desires to the other party. Our currents of affection chase one another to the heavens, circling and bouncing off seventh Chakra, vortexing to the skies. Our love races up Jacob's ladder reaching out to angels, ancestors, kindred souls and the most high. Drawing them back to us for guidance, direction, support and wisdom so without ever taking one step we follow them through the corridors of love. For the first time I've come to experience love. I now understand its peace, inspiration, and desire without want, release of control while maintaining complete and total control. Briefly my eyes close and I gaze, stare deeper into us looking without sight falling

deeper into self opening doors to you that I'd not opened yet

myself, but then again how could I when you are the key. Trailing

the feel of insight that is intuitive knowledge I find that time has

raced to this very moment to enjoy the purity of us. As it stretches

the very fabric of self with a great inhale and held breath so that

it may also remember where it was when this took place, hoping

that we may out endure its essence. Eyes open I realize that you

move me beyond orbital planes to where I truly belong which is

exactly where I am now.

Chocolate Silk

It's more than the way her body moves it's the way her body

moves me

Beyond temptations desire to a state simply

Described as affectionate bliss

Transferred through the convection of lips

As my hands descend to the direction of hips

Our tongues tied in one another's grips

Two bodies moving beyond what's real

Too softly her skins mellow feel

Calling for the comfort of my embrace

Falling into confrontations grip of the passionate chase

Of my palms to her waist, my fingers to her thighs

My tongue's pursuit of her taste, as my ears stalk her sighs

Through every fondle, grip, grasp, and grope

Enjoying each touch, grab, slurp, and stroke

Of her softly tender, hotly tempered

Erotically moist seduction that has me rendered

Helpless, hopeless lost in lust and guilt

Addicted to the warmth of her chocolate silk

Something Romantic

Silhouettes tussle with familiarity amidst a candle lit room

As our bodies overcome introductions awkwardness and find the
perfect position for passion to be consumed

The flutter of your eyes, the coyness of your grin

All signs of approval pointing to letting me in

To your mind's fantasies and your reality's seduction

Two silhouettes wrapped tightly one smiling one blushing

Warm oils and my fingertips sensually caressing your skin

As your body comes to know the feel of heavenly sin

From neck to shoulder to hips to waist

My hands outlined beauty as your body is traced

By the caressing adoration of my touch

As you succumb to my fingers strokes and my tongue's clutch

Our embrace moves beyond midnights chimes

Tonight let's seek and find pleasures weak spots

As orgasm scribbles out tales of forget we not's

The Corner of Seduction & Pleasure

Don't talk just listen to pleasure's exhales

As I listen to your body's desires with attentive detail

Learning how you like to be gently touched and caressed

Desired and admired as you're slowly undressed

Slurped neck to thigh and fondled tenderly

My tongue and honey across your breast began sending the

Chills of passion up and down your spine

But it was my poetry's recital that captured your mind

The slow grind of my words mental imagery

Seductively the initial thought that lead to physical sensation

Of my tongue across your body which lead to initial penetration

Of being in your space making you hot

My palms grasping your waist as I stroke your spot

Mentally, physically, spiritually, emotionally

Discreetly, completely, satisfying you, proportionally

To the same amount of pleasure you're giving me

Back and forth pleasure at its peak

17

A rare mix of carnal, erotic, spiritual soft love making so unique

Nickels Awareness

Watch me: Watching you, the sleek line of your waist, the way you stroll stalking passion like a cat on the prowl, eyeing you from a far, peering closely into an addiction of mind body and soul.

Feel me, Feeling you: Understand I'm addicted to your sophistication. How I can relate to the subtle aggressiveness of your personality the sheer intimacies of you.

Taste me, tasting you: The honey dipped pleasure of your desires. Caramel cravings yearning to dine on appetizers of eye contacts, lip locks, and serpentine tongue grasps on your clit. The main course being the way you relax inviting my full penetration. Dessert the warmth of your sugared walls raining torrential down pours of your juices down my thighs.

Stop listen to the…Shh listen, to your sirenesque sighs indulging, calling me to stroke your passion deeper, harder longer. I hear the tremors, convulsions and earthquakes of your sensuality faulting from your thighs to stomach to the trembling screams of my name. There? Right there is that the spot?

You want me to stroke it from what angle? I need not ask, I can hear it in your body language. The way your walls converse with my manhood through sign language...Palpation, pulsation, contraction and erotic expulsion: You, me, we indulging in rising echoes of climax.

The aroma of stimulation followed you into the room. Quick thrusts, wind gusts of cinnamon apple desire exhaled through tongue and inhaled through lungs as we exchange kisses from neck to cheek to lips. Clouds raining caramelized shavings of fantasy entice me to leave marshmallow tongue prints down your back. I step back to take a deep breath. I know you smell it too. It's the overwhelmingly subtle seductive fragrance of total arousal topped with MM MM good and sprinkles of damn you know I like it like that, can I have some more? Simply stated, you and I an ice cream sundae mocha-latte dream.

Fetish part 1

Let me be your fixation. The reason you rush home on your lunch break searching for what satisfies your hunger. An appetizing course of my lips on your neck my hands on your hips and your stomach's tremors to the rhythm of my stroke. It is what it is. One hour of time standing still and allowing us to grace the celestial planes of orgasm with our sensual flavors of chocolate tootsie popped escapades. Just how many strokes of your lips on my tip, my tongue on your clit, you riding up and down grinding back and forth will it take to get to the center of climax? I don't know but it could never be enough to satisfy my desire to please you, my desire to satisfy you, my desire to leave you laying there motionless overwhelmed from our encounter craving more of my brown sugar caned sweet dick injections. As soon as you recover from the pleasure we just shared you'd wake up to my lips on your lips, my tongue on your clit, the back wall grinding sensation of me causing your walls to throb in pleasure's paradise as you convulse through an awakening of stimulation

You must be my obsession. What gets me through the long boring days at work are the thoughts of our nightly encounters amidst scented candles and the moonlit shadows of our bodies meeting in the center of the room. The naked truth unveils the fact that we've both become consumed by arousal. Your nipples erect from the warmth of my mouth, your waters flowing from the strokes of my tongue from thigh to lips and back again. Imagine pre-cum coating me from tip to base from my encounter with the erotic texture of your mouth. Our shadows anticipate the next move of our fleshly desires anxiously awaiting the seductive feel of me diving head first into the warmth of your oceans waters. Picture me stroking your passion causing tidal waves of pleasure to rise beyond your shores as you wonder "Damn why does this night ever have to end?

Let's indulge in one another taking the time to enjoy the core of one another's sensuality. I can tell you enjoy how I take control sliding you into freakish positions that you never imagined possible all the while sliding me in you deep to the left, hard from the right and intensely from the back causing your walls to conform to the shape of me. As your orgasmic juices erupt and slide down my manhood. I enjoy the clutch of you grasping at me with each down stroke, convulsing with each momentum gaining thrust of my chocolate hammer pounding away at your sensuality striking, beating, pounding, and pummeling your spot. Yeah that spot right there the one that sends tremors from your thighs to stomach bringing on head changes and body numbness. I thoroughly enjoy the feel of your athletically soft ass bouncing back to me, rippling to the rhythm of my strokes coinciding with my hands on your hips and your fists full of sheets. Damn I can never get enough.

Fetish 2

Sensually seductive your picturesque frame

Subtly tempting me calling my name

I hear your hips faded whispers

Their sway leading us to X-Rated ventures

Convincingly, whole heartedly, coaxing me

Into allowing the pleasures of your lips hosting me

Beyond the chocolate fields of passion

Silhouettes entangled in joy with plans of lasting

Through the introduction of caressing

Satisfaction until its contractions leads to undressing

Inhibition, allowing the intermission

Of twisting and shifting until we find the perfect position

For giving your pleasure more pleasure than it can handle

As sensuality faint of breath slowly pants to

The tempo of our grind your hips slow wind

The perfect intoxication of our meeting minds

Carnal Desires

Deep, filling, intense, insertions

Late night's potential passion to early morning's kinetic pleasure

conversions

The graceful stroke of my fingers across your skin

Multiple shadows contorting to blend

Into heavy breathing, steady freaking orgasmic formations

Brought on by thigh trembling, sigh vending sensations

Imagine me finding your spot

Pleasures friction grinding you hot

Passions addiction climbing on top

Overwhelmed by the moment you crying don't stop

I know you like hard, pounding, pummeling strokes

Tongue's tip from neck to breast to stomach to thigh leaving you

soaked

Lost in lip biting, grip tightening anticipation

Waiting on all night tongue to clit, hands on hips doggy style
confrontations

Through a back arching, throat parching night of sin

As we succumb to climax again and again

Vision our passions conversing

Seeking climax through rehearsing

Exploring one another's erotic perversions

Drowning in the bliss of orgasmic submersions

Tell Me

Lady let me learn your secrets. The intimate details of your

passions desires. Your body whispering to mine through actions

of torso wrapping stomach convulsing lip biting moments. It's

conveying the heat of your sensuality linguistically as beads of

sweat slide down your spine forming an erotic river calling me to

stroke your every desire. My tongue circling your belly button

enticing you to tell me more, tell me how you find joy in

repetition. You love the repetition of me slurping you from thighs

to lips from lips to clit from clit back to lips and from lips back to

clit on to the gentle insertion of my tongue as the subtle

contractions of your thighs tell me that you want to tell me more.

Tell me how you crave the sigh indulging tongue curdling

injections of my manhood. Your sighs now a babbling brook of

inexpressible unimagined pleasure. It's no secret that you like it

from behind, the arch in your back the gateway leading to

stimulation. The rippling of your ass cheeks a caramelized tidal

wave of seduction crashing against my firmness, a firmness

causing you to release your sultry warmth of honey dew nectar.

Love's Angel

A blessing from God bestowed on me to nurture cherish and

satisfy. Imagine us parasailing on winds from the lungs of the

most high beyond the monotony of everyday stress. To a paradise

of solitude where all that matters is you and I getting off on us.

Ms. Chocolate martini, honey glazed perfection slide into my cup

and let me slowly sip the essence of you until I become

intoxicated with loves desire to pleasure you again and again.

We'll experience a happy hour that lasts a life time. So Ms. Butter

scotched tootsie roll allow me to unwrap the pleasure that is you

and learn your mannerisms. How many licks does it take? To

overcome the awkwardness of introductions and formalities and

become familiar with a love that is the addiction of lungs to air.

Vision the sun smiling on us in envy of the warmth of our

embraces as our souls become one. You and I a caramel coated

figurine hand carved by the most high for all future lovers to

emulate.

Love's Blessing

Tonight chose us. As love's angels harmonize the song of our consummation stars light the path to complete elation and the moon sheds caramelized tears of heavens dew. Caramelized tears of heavens dew become water falling rivers of joy cascading fairytales of love into our reality. Our souls two step to the drum of happiness ascending to cloud 9 on the feathers of cupid's wings. The winds of passion hush and ride the gusts of our torso wrapping hand in hand love making. The perfect syncopation of our hearts pounding out one resounding beat of don't ever let the night end.

How am I worthy of making love to an angel?

I must be God's favorite son

How am I worthy of being blessed with a love so precious?

I must be God's favorite son

This moment chose you and I. The hands of time stand still allowing me to run my hands from cheeks to hips. I know I've done this a thousand times but every time I stand still, adoring the beauty that is you. Slow motion tidal waves slosh back and forth as I swim in an ocean of your love. Diving deeper into the fathoms of your mellow warmth, the depths of your liquid love. Sands of the hour glass pause admiring the way our bodies come together perfectly as one caramel coated figurine of ecstasy, a figurine hand carved by heaven, personally blown and molded by the most high for all future lovers to aspire to. Our bodies together form a road map to love's pinnacle discreetly signed by God.

How am I worthy of being loved by an angel?

I must be God's favorite son

How am I worthy of being blessed with a love so precious?

I must be God's favorite son

First Sight

First glance momentary eye contact and yet an everlasting picturesque vision of a masterpiece sat in my mind. We stood alone in a crowded room engulfed in a thunderstorm. Surrounded by the thunder of crowds wondering if in a midnight's rain I could stand drenched by the cotton candy sweet passion of you.

Double take I can't believe this coke bottle shaped breath of fresh air has blown in like the wind and aroused my five senses. My sense of taste, I long to taste the erogenous zones of you slurped across my taste buds and cream along my tongue. My sense of touch now has the gentle touch of walls pounding, pulsating and palpating around my paintbrush which strokes with the precision of Van Gogh. My ears long for the soft subtle moans of your sensuality calling me to quench the thirst of your lava like hot pools that swell to the rhythm of my symphonic harmony until your volcano over flows from the melody that we create.

Eyes closed I step back to catch my righteousness. Behold I have become lost in you the gospel, heavens girl the lost commandment to put it modestly you are a caramel glazed honey brushed recreation of perfection. Regaining my composure I slowly make my way towards you hoping that our eye contact will lead to the contact of two desires meeting on the streets of stimulation in a high speed collision that leads to our frames being wrapped tightly.

Visions of a vision I stand before you overcoming the awkwardness of introductions. We engage in conversation but not just mere conversation. I mean deep rich titillating sultry words roll from your tongue and massage the cerebral core of my mind. In return I offer soothing dialect that wraps my lips around the pearls of your thoughts while my tongue increasingly strokes your minds hot spots. You lead I follow and you openly say. "In the beginning there was two." I reply "I was Adam and Eve was you." You say "If I nourish your soul." I reply "I will harvest the desires of your essence." as we stand crowdedly in an empty room.

Dangerous

Her body's curves winding to the direction of addiction I became addicted to the shape of her frame. A picturesque stature of sultry perfection, her shoulders to spine sloping to the beauty of the small of her back which is a cocoa stem holding the ripeness of her plum shaped ass. Her thighs envied by shapely thickness, the tone of her voice the song of sirens drawing me nearer to her shores. How could I resist? Her conversation is the temptation of chocolate covered quick sand inviting me to dive in head first. Engulfed by her words I'd become breathless in awe of the moment. Her sensuality was a double agent working for me allowing me to become closer to her all the while working for her to bring me to a climactic state of vulnerability and indeed I was vulnerable, consumed by the moment taken by the pleasures of her body's sensations. The sensation of her tongue was a warm blade piercing the armor of my arousal moving from neck to chest to stomach and back leaving my excitement exposed. Her mouth was the warmth of the amazons rain sensually torrentially caressing my passion with a constant down pour of "Get it up,

give it up, I'll get it off again and again and again." The rhythm of

her bouncing it back to me was the high speed chase of two cars

speeding down a one way street in the wrong direction bumper to

grille touching, pounding and exchanging paint in the pursuit of

ecstasy.

Full Circle

One night stand, that's what we agreed upon six hours of no string uninhibited wall sweating window fogging unadulterated passion. However pictures of you in that red thong reminiscent of you sliding up and down, see sawing on my playgrounds thick hard as steel pole of ecstasy the sound of your ass slapping, clapping against me drumming out an instrumental of passion seductively nasty like a Marvin Gaye, R Kelly collaboration brought me back to you.

Second chance encounter; was it by mistake or by fate that the fork in this road called lust would bring our paths together again. Our passions race tit for tat. My tongue hugs the highways of your swirling, winding curvaceous body. As it accelerates into the apex of your sensuality, you wrap your lips around my stick shifting from first to fifth. You've got my mind clutching, braking, racing as we speed down this Audubon of stimulation.

Third time's a charm: One more night of sheet drenching, bed bouncing and wall climbing sex. You are my instrument of choice. A beautifully finished mahogany piano. My fingers gently caressed your erotic ebony keys creating a tone called Convulsion. My strokes urged you to release your ivory symphonic seduction. Eighth, quarter whole notes perfect chords of my name sighed by you in a crescendo of climax.

Complete and total addiction: intoxicating sugar cane to my minds sweet tooth how did it come to this? You are my chocolate coated tear drop, the sweetest sadness. I love the intimate emotional moments we share. I loathe seeing you leave. I fiend for your touch, the way you cream to my clutch. Woman will you be mine forever?

Morris Gamble

Motions of Love

Wings fluttered flaps wisps gusts of pollen

Sweet nectar divine brings bees calling

Nervous, anxious moments of anticipation

Honey suckled kisses of you please don't keep me waiting

Babbling brooks subtle ripples are unfathomed

Molding shores into shapes that they've never imagined

The refreshing depths of you a stimulating verbal bliss

Arms and heart open I've never felt like this

Untethered ascents of climax on wings of your presence

Free falling from mountains becoming lost in your essence

Uninhibited rising emotion our passions tangle

Uncontrollable highs have me falling in love with an angel

Algebraic equations reveal the alignment

Two way mirror reflects a Royal consignment

The mathematical perfection of you plus I equals perfect
symmetry

As King recognizes Queen standing in the proper proximity

Fractured code of pounding admiration

Never ending hour glass sands drips adoration

The broken silence of my heart cries tears of trust

And perpetually love will revolve around us

Pleasure's Angel

Her touch incited arousal as if her fingers were the keys to my excitement. Each finger tipped stroke gliding from heavens temptation to my soul's desires and back. Opening another door of unknown joy. It was almost as if she was more in tune with my passion than I was myself. Slowly she mounted me and slid her womanhood from my stomach to penis to thigh. I could feel the warmth of her moisture through her panties. An even tempered furnace of cotton candied soft pleasure, a sudden tropical storm on the beach with the sun still out. The feel of her body all over mine simply stated a humidity of pleasure, a warm sensation of intoxication suffocating my inhibitions. There I was lost in her Bermuda of teasing, stroking and groping which was a triangle of seduction taking me to a cusp of insatiability from which I did not want to return.

Raw Emotion

For the last several months I've loved you from a far

Passionate poems multi colored roses I'd placed on your car

Knowing what we know, we know we could never go back

But I adore your essence and the woman you are I'll always love

that

I don't want to waste yours or mine but I want to take the time

To learn your womanhood and pick your mind

I mean ask some questions simply addressing

If we can become a little closer no time for second guessing

I'm stressing a relationship on how two souls relate

Not so much falling in love but being in love, let me set things

straight

I love all the time we'd spend

Intimately, unromantically friends

Kissing cousins hand in hand and we need not speak

A formality of our reality closer than cheek to cheek

It started with fast laughs and long chuckles

Honey suckled

Strolls along the beach, chilling in the park soul to soul deeply

rooted conversation

This we nurtured and cherished and so would bloom and

carnation

A friendship that would flourish through thorns to petals

When the dust rises or settles I'll never forget you

Or turn my back

I'm more concerned with facts

Of how you're doing

What you're pursuing

Simple things like that

And you adore the fact

That I can finish your sentence

I cherish you for who you are in every single instance

You can be you around me nothing more and nothing less

Suffocation through separation because I'm breathing your breaths

CPR techniques that keep love flowing from lungs to heart to brain

Companions Passionately Resuscitating love again and again

It's far more than sex and I'm so much more than your man

A confidant, lover and shoulder who in hard times offers a hand

Aijahn Bleu: The Color of (Part 1)

What is Aijahn Bleu: The color of orgasmic pleasure, a hue of tongue curdling body numbing breath shortening erotic satisfaction. A color so deep it will stroke the inner most portion of your soul causing you to release tears of joy. A quiet storm of your moans, sighs, involuntary scream zigzagging down the windows. It is a color that will have you climbing walls as your walls palpate in a resounding echo of thunderous passion.

Who is Aijahn bleu: The color of sensuality. The soothing relaxation of a bubbling Jacuzzi caressing your mind with the sultry jet streamed flow of my words. The verbal harmony of the ocean molesting the shore as the moonlight dances the samba on waves of seduction.

I am Aijahn Bleu: The color of your fantasy. A chocolate dream plucked from the depths of your mind, emerging from the midst of your subconscious to massage your minds hot spots. Here I am no longer a figment of your imagination but the knee weakening, thigh trembling, stomach convulsing, mind blowing spiritual flesh of your fantasy's desires.

Aijahn Bleu: The color of (part 2)

What is Aijahn Bleu?

The color of heaven's lust

An intimate connection of soul to soul causing the heavens to
blush

The sweet divinity of Eden's crush

The joy of heavenly sin which is my tongues touch

Celestial bodies on an erotic crash course

I'll stroke your pearled gate with more passion that it really
supports

Indulging your body to scream until your passion is hoarse

Who is Aijahn Bleu?

The color of addictions intoxication

The joy that's felt by repetitive sensations

My tongue gyrating on your pearl, your pearl shivering and
shaking

Your clit rising and falling to my tongues vibrations

Your body drunken with passion body numb mind light

Freaking under the influence chasing pleasure feeling like

You don't want the morning to interrupt the night

I am Aijahn Bleu

The color of uncertainty

Uncertain you can handle contradictive addictions

Cooling your body with the heat of my tongue's friction

Not saying a word communicating through our body's diction

The way you return to this strangers feel

Loving you differently every time but with a familiar appeal

As you drift off to fantasy's paradise but cum for what is so
real

Quicksand

It began with the initial eye contact

Flirtatious batting of your eyes

Polar opposites we attract

Drawn to the feel of passions rise

The full soft shape of your lips

An erotic invitation

The sultry sway of your hips

Thoughts of intimate conversation

Pulling me in, having me thinking

Could we be friends, woman I'm sinking

Honey suckled introductions

Of pleasurable exchanges

Blue prints of constructions

Of a love to outlast the ages

Withstand the test of time

Endure abrasions of change

Contoured by satisfactions mind

Through it all our love remains

As I descend, my resistance is none

Perhaps more than friends, we can be one

The grips of your walls

The warmth of your river

Your sighs gentle calls

The feel of thighs quiver

The sketch of nails on my back

Nibbles upon bottom lip gently

Down strokes that resound in echoing smacks

Woman you're simply

Pulling me in, having me thinking

Don't let this end, woman I'm sinking

Seduction

Imagine the lulled whispers of sensuality bouncing off the reeds, resounding into the mesmerizing chant of "Let me explore all of your fantasies" as we float down the Nile by moonlight, the heat of the summers' night enhanced by the warmth of my touch, my fingers massaging from the small of your back up to your shoulders. Just relax into the comfort of my embrace because tonight however you want it you shall have it. Come to me; allow me to find the secrets of your pleasure as you succumb to the aroma of curiosity. I'll stroke your mental, physical and emotional desires until your pleasure begins to quiver. Exposing exactly what it is that your body yearns for. Sensually teasing it until you give me permission to take advantage of the moment let me erase all of your maybes because tonight there is no room for them at all. Nor is there room for doubt, there is only room for the intimate feel of my fingers trickling down your spine as the sands of the hour glass drip one by one in slow motion to the pace of my slurps outlining your hips and tracing your waist line causing you to squirm in delight and when the hour glass runs empty and you think you've had enough I'll flip it over and enjoy your pleasures again. Listen carefully to the tone of my sheets calling your name in the melodic tone of A major. Close your eyes and ride the harmony of your body being cloaked in pleasure, caressed by its own desire to be fondled by a touch so soothing that relaxation becomes overwhelmed with envy. Don't try to fight it because it is what it is. Exactly what it shall be is my touch wrapping your body in a cradle of satisfaction until your cravings are lullabied.

You're going to make me

You're going to make me get grown in here, the way you are stalking passion. Lights off, moonlight peering through the shades, the aroma of cinnamon apple candles filled the room. The Isley Brothers Don't Say Goodnight playing in the background, all the subtle subliminal suggestions pointing to a night of seduction.

You're going to make me lose control the way you're up and down rollercoaster riding this dick. At the height of stimulation teasing me with small circular motions around the tip, strategically and erotically carefully making sure I remain in you. Not allowing me to explode sliding up and down my shaft leaving it coated with your liquid nectar passion. You're transitioning from the gentle up and down motion to the vigorous pounding of your ass cheeks against me.

You're going to make me put my tongue on you. All of that milk chocolate wrapped tightly sophisticatedly sexy in that lingerie. The softness of your breasts screaming to me, "melt me with the heat of your tongue." Slowly making my way to your hips slurping on to the Milky Way sweetness of your lips kissing lapping licking outer to inner until I find the Tootsie Popped flavor of your clit, tonight indeed we shall find out how many licks it takes.

You're going to make me come back for more. The naked

truth of you is a chocolate brushed alluring enticing addiction. I find myself needing you. An orgasmic freaky fix that I could never get enough of, the perfect combination of erotic sophisticated intelligent freak.

Soon

For one night

Submerge into bliss

Tongue tied

Immersed in a kiss

No rush

Let's touch

Every spot in the room

As I touch each spot that consumes

Your passion, your pleasure

More action, more feathered

Strokes of tongue across thighs

Gropes that cause sighs

To emerge in the light

As our desires converse in the night

Leading to mental pictures

Conveyed through gentle whispers

Of erotic melodies

Your forbidden fantasies

Your body telling me

That I'm giving what you need

Something intensely deep

Abruptly rough

Immense and steep

Just enough

Long slow grinds with no pauses

Fast hard strokes that causes

Legs quivers, pleasures impatience

Stomach shivers, breaths faintness

Long convulsions, expressions blankness

Warm expulsions, orgasms acquaintance

Still Dreaming

Last night's dream

A fantasy of us

God's finger painted scene

The embodiment of trust

Hand in hand walking on water

Firmly standing a top God's shoulders

Knowing that we can't falter

As long as we let his love mold us

Into the perfect figurine

The beauty of the most highs impression

The chance to have held, lived and seen

Love in its purest form more than a blessing

The sun's slow ascent

Left the sky a shade of periwinkle

Merely mirroring the event

Of your eyes warming twinkle

Setting flame to my soul

As the sun does the skies

With a tender warming glow

Bringing passion to a rise

The gentle whispers of the wind

Urge us to move nearer

Become lost in the feel of pleasure's skin

Passions subtly calling us and I can hear her

Guiding us to the direction

To the cliffs of bliss a top love's cove

Below splashed the waters of affection

So into the Lord's hands we dove

Head first into something infinite

Only to awaken to the joy of your kiss

Our souls engaged in something intimate

A connection created in the halls of eternal bliss

The Art of Touching

Finger painted strokes

Slightly tainted gropes

Of my hands across your hips

The slow circular trips

From stomach, to waist, to thighs

Become my palms chase of sighs

Simple sensual descent slowly winding

Into complicated intoxicating maneuvers grinding

Of body wrapping torso clasping

Lip locked ass grasping

Chest to breast amaretto sips

Of my tongue and ice from breast to clit

Reverberated through the way you're moist

Regurgitated joy in the tremors of your voice

We become trapped in pleasures grips

Imagine your pearl being stroked by tongue's tip

Engulfed by lips suction

Overwhelmed by the warm seduction

Sensual bodies kiss

Framed to perfection by the bliss

Of mahogany post, satin sheets

Scented candles, the moon's peeps

Through our curtains

As we're flirting

Like the sensual caress of ocean to shore

Dashing retreating, crashing receding until I find what you adore

Less of more or more of less

Provocative grope or sensual caress

Don't speak a word

One simple verb

I'll listen to your body's reactions

In addition to pleasure there's the simple subtraction

Of stress and drama

See I believe in karma

So I want to touch you like you need to be touched

Love reciprocated perfectly, genuinely unrushed

Conveyed by the heavens hush

And pleasure it takes in our body's touch

Iced Black Honey

The essence of you is soothing with no regrets. Your conversation drip dropped an even flow of thick rich creamy "Hey don't you want to know the pleasure of heavens sweetness." Drawing me nearer like a moth to a cinnamon honey scented candle light in the pitch black night. Natures' nectar the soft feel of your skin next to mine, taking my passions to the brink of fantasy's desire. My thoughts drifting to forbidden pleasures of lollipop dreams of you poured slowly onto my sheets, melting from the heat of passion, conforming to the shape of my tongue, as my taste buds dancing to the erotically sinful taste of your thighs. Imagine my lips sticky from becoming intimate with your sugared pearl of sensuality. My sheets now a honey combed haven for stimulation. The subtle rise and fall of your hips is sheer intoxication and the cold gusts of your seduction sends chills down my spine taking me to the threshold of lust. Brain Freeze! How did it come to this, me becoming captivated by the ice cold addiction

that is you.

T.K.O.

We squared off in the center of the ring

Undisputed champ versus number one contender

We proceeded to exchange blows at the bells first ding

She had been known to make a few challengers surrender

But I was in it for the duration of the bout

Besides it was only the first round

My tongue's jabs across her was for feeling her out

My blows to her body were for slowing her down

Second round I'm checking now for a couple of things

Is she breathing heavy what's the motion of her hips?

My defenses still up I parried her swings

Made my move because now she's giving me access to her lips

Upper cut, jab, hook, she threw a flurry of blows

Clean head shots as she stroked with her left

Worked my way off the ropes and got back on my toes

Shuffled to buy time and got right with my breath

She had hand speed, head speed, perfect in rhythm

The peoples champ in her arena with savvy and flash

But I was off the ginseng heavy bag so I wasn't tripping

As I hit her with a straight right and talked a little trash

You want that, take that, tell me how you like that

I swung haymaker after haymaker going in for the kill

Trying to put that thing on her until she couldn't fight back

And I could tell by her reaction that she was losing her will

Briefly her eyes closed, she let loose a sigh

I knew the time had come to put her away

As her knees slightly buckled through convulsion of thigh

What's my name? Whose is it? But she couldn't say

Riskily I decided to go for it all now

Her stomach trembled, legs quivered through one final collapse

She curled into the fetal position and threw in the towel

As the former champ gave in to climax

T.K.O. (Rematch)

Tonight was going to be a bit different. I could feel the electricity in the air as she disrobed I tried not to stare overtly. However she carried that five foot ten, one hundred fifty eight pound frame perfectly. There was no time for feeling one another out, we got straight down to business. My strategy was to stick and move. I mean hit her with a quick flurry of intense strokes and move on to the next angle. She stalked my passion, cutting off the ring offering her cheeks as a target. Pleading, begging me to hit it…faster and harder! Until she had me backed in a corner, daring me to swing my way out of the grips of pleasure she continued to stalk me. In an instance everything began to move in slow motion. My thighs trembled and a bead of sweat hit the canvas. Down I went to the dew of her excitement, sipping on the ambrosia of her passion, while I received a low blow that would send the average man to the showers early. After a count of somewhere between 6 and 9, maybe it was a standing 8 we were right back at it. Checking myself to make sure my glove was tight I headed in aggressively. Side to side, back and forth pleasantries were exchanged. Soon the rules of engagement were out the door as we exploded into a no holds barred anything goes frenzy of body numbing bliss. On we continued through the night, beyond the rising of the sun on to exhaustion. As we both laid on the matt with the sheets of our desires unveiled.

Watercolors

Your sleek blackened silhouette calls to me, outlined by the early morning's midnight Blue.

Enhanced by the iridescent yellow glow of the moon that peers through my curtain.

My fingertips yearn to be dipped in the deep brown shades of ebony that is you. The

white satin sheets of my canvas scream for the golden sighs of your consummation to be

stroked across its pages. Causing midnights blue to convulse and mix with the rising suns

reds, creating a purple of passion so intense that we both collapse into a deep foggy grey

slumber. Only to awaken to a masterpiece created by the multi-faceted colors of our love.

Softly

Vulnerable

Insatiable

Moments that you're aroused

Slurping on your body with ice in my mouth

Moaning, sighing, whining your may as well shout

Passions friction melts your body from inside out

No doubt…

I'm feeling you,

And I can feel the dew

Of passion in the air so don't be scared to

Be assertive aggressive

We're flirting progressive

To higher stages of freaking

In body language we're speaking

Won't you teach me some lessons (on you)

It's only me in your presence (us two)

Lip to lip

While I sip,

Slurp suckle your essence

Groping, grabbing, shifting, twisting

Every freaky position

And what I'm missing

Is you in subtle states of submission

And what I vision

Are premonitions of your oceans over flow

Waves rise to the undertow

Of me stroking to and fro

Back and forth, in and out, up and down

Make those sounds

You like the way it's going down

And they need not know how

I can make your body smile

Baby girl I truly vow

Intimate encounters

Me and you in the shower

Sunken tub bubble baths

Making love's aftermath

My tongue across your body would feel like iced satin

The moon would turn green in envy of our passion

Surpassing orgasmic

A–U–T–Omatic

Fulfilling every candy coated dream you ever imagined

Have you fathomed?

Having your body convulse

To the pulse

Of my strokes

Head changing

Legs shaking

Breath taking

Now were making

Progress

I'm just

Lost in you

Your imaginations' figment

Here solely to

Touch you

Tease you

Tempt you

Please you

Undress you

Ease you

Caress you

Relieve you

Final Destination

Early morning text, evening calls, late night sext, in an attempt to gain full disclosure of exactly how you like it. Don't tell me what I want to hear tell me what I need to hear. What I need to hear is that I can be the custodian of your excitement, pleasure, happiness and dreams. I promise to keep track of every record, while we set new records of passion and accomplish feats never attempted before. Don't worry I'll brush, dust, feather, stroke every nook, cranny and corner, be your pillar of strength and greatest support. All you have to do is hand me the keys sit back and watch me caress every tumbler taking your mind through numbing, tumbling, head changes back and forth across the planes of sensuality's sensations in and out of the twelve dimensions of orgasm. I know you may have experienced the first two: Physical and Mental but allow me to be your guide through the next ten beginning with the spiritual. I know they say everything is only temporary and this is true but let's place temporary in a quandary by lining temporary pleasure up back to back to back so many times that it extends beyond forever. Foreplay-ever changing switching and repositioning until temporary fits next to temporary completing your jig saw puzzle's GROANED rebuttal of satisfaction so that I may see the complete picture of your fantasy's hopes blooming into a reality. Then lets live it out, bend it about 180 degrees so we can go straight from point A to point B. Point A being this fantasy and Point B being the next but along the way we stop 179 times to redefine the limits of Euphoria. Exultation rises in your hips its surprise is in my lips upon neck stomach inner thighs; its surprise and subtle highs are in my trips to your waters depths, altered breaths and perfect meeting of our minds. I'll keep your dreams a secret just let me frequent the celestial fields of your subconscious unaware it's just in different forms of pleasure being replayed again and again. Let me be Joseph and interpret for you. The one of you falling with no end in sight, that's about your desire to fall so deeply in love with me that you'll never touch the monotony of an average lover again and you continue to fall because you're waiting for the moment we meet. The one about the caterpillar in the empty garden trapped in the rain, now that entails a little more depth.

The caterpillar symbolizes a young love that hasn't fully matured basically you and I. The garden being empty is the caterpillar starving for the nourishment of a love that will bloom into something that can provide her protection from the relentless down pour of disappointment that muddies the grounds of security. Let me protect, nourish and provide you with the love you've been missing and I promise you will Soar to heights you've never imagined. The dream of us sharing a bottle of wine and me devouring your pleasure until the night gives way to the sun. Well that's about us sharing a bottle of wine and me devouring your passions until the night gives way to the sun.....

Perfection

Passion flickers in your eyes. They gleam as erotic candles

lighting the way to your thighs, your hips erotic handles molded

to the formation of my hands. Your rhythm a chocolate coated

cobble stoned street bouncing back and forth to and fro to the

intersection of pleasure and climax. How can I entice you to ride

with me down this road affectionately known as arousals

consummation, you won't regret this. Relax into the warmth of

my tongue as I succumb to the succulence of you. I have

intentions of making tonight one you won't soon forget. A legend

of such epic it will be passed down from mothers to daughters for

generations.

Imagine us intertwined from bed to floor to hallway, kitchen

counter, ripping on my tippy toes. Beads of my sweat race down your chest, sheets soaked, your walls palpating, pulsating to my strokes. We lay chest to back my lips on your neck. Tempo: slow grind, long strokes, intense convulsion as you try to capture your breath. Your lips quiver at conversation racing to catch, express the thoughts of your mind, the pleasures of your body's experience, the tingling of your erogenous zones the warmth in your soul, the lava like hot pools swirling erupting between your thighs again and again. Yet as the same time cold chills racing up and down your spine. My tongue across your body would feel like a hot summer night wrapped in iced satin sheets. Lay there, be my canvas as my tongue Picasso's a picture of caramelized rain falling from clear skies into an ocean of warm desire, the desire to please you in every way possible as we become one.

Morris Gamble

Harmony

You in that lingerie simply edible

A caramel apple dream it's so incredible

I know the look on my face was more than legible

Hieroglyphic maybe Akkadian perhaps it said to you

You're my addiction

Unsure confliction

Between love and lust

My chocolate coated pacification

Matter of fact my body's still shaking

From you taking me to passions cusp

The way you walked through the door compelled this

Sensuality filled the room I know you can smell it

The feel of your lips on my neck slightly more than Angelic

It would sound something like this if my body could tell it

I've become overwhelmed by your insatiable pleasures

Liquid gold flowing form platinum lips it seems your body's my treasure

Caught in the moment I'm feeling the rush

Satisfaction becomes overjoyed and releases a tear

Orgasmic delight pauses and cups its' ear

As pleasure fondles its self to the sounds of us

Crosswalk

Back At It

My teenage years stressed but carefree

I still consider myself blessed to barely

See graduation so many peers didn't make it

Copper streets, wooden dreams their golden souls couldn't take it

Lost and still searching for a hustlers Oasis

Pain, struggle, fame, hustle and death all wear similar faces

Lead to similar places traveling the same roads

My heart aches empty for what my desire still holds

A similar story has been told yet we're still driven to hustling

The black sheep, outcasts, veterans of creative suffering

Is it enough when chalk lines lead to miniature caskets?

Poverty stricken kings misled by the fastest

Ways to get money selling their souls for paper

Exchanging their riches for the drama of capers

My eyes awaken each morning never knowing what the day

brings

Poverty, prostitution, the struggle, my hustle still surrounded by
the same things

Praying for blessings upon my child a ray of hope and peace of
mind

Greeted by the misfortune of inner city living I'm still gripping
my nine

Hoping no troubles shall find me but that's not reality

God please forgive me for my sins they're a mere formality

Of searching for the means to find the right direction

With you as my shield of faith, my sword a hustlers discretion

To get it like I need it, still be a street soldier

Live right by you, carry the world on my shoulders

Everyday I'm confronted by conflict my pain screams from its exit
wounds

My bandages are twenty inch rims I guess the Jaguar is my tomb

Still consumed by material dreams the fast life and women

My life contains variable scenes of stress, strife, losing and
winning

Sinning since beginning searching for the right punctuation

To end my life: period, question mark, or exclamation

Point blank will they question the value of my life or scream my
name as a Martyr

In revolutions for peace, equality, upliftment somebody's got to

Understand I've taught and coached trying to reach the youth

While fighting my own demons gulping something 80 proof

Intoxicated by the dreams of seeing their success

A corner stone through their struggles praying for more and less

More blessings, less struggles, more carries, less fumbles

More chances to get it without dropping it while still remaining
humble

Once I get it, forget it, I'm never letting go

And if before it get, if I've missed it and my wind has left slow

Bestow these blessings on my seeds through knowledge of self

Manifest wisdom of gold so that they may chase true wealth.

Ms. Green Light

15 years and they finally placed a light in her intersection

The first to use it was a boy on a bike with no elbow, chin, and knee or head protection

Back and forth he crossed her lines a couple of times

Stumbling through wheelies and things as he learned how to grind

As time moved and grew so did her fetish

As pedestrian traffic added her block to its credits

You could trace the stroll of lovers and friends between her lines

But the footsteps of an athlete always seemed to find

The perfect rhythm and gate to make all traffic wait

As her guard for crossing slept and inhibition somehow escaped

She loved the way big rims and low profile tires caressed her curves

And how a sagging thug in bandanna could bring the hood to her suburbs

Not disturbed in the least of how her road became a street

From 2 lanes to a 3 way intersection women began to creep

Jaguar, Cougar, Sable cat fight damn near fatal

As they swerved through oncoming traffic and barely were able

To avoid the big rig big wig boyfriend slash asshole

Who taught her how to make quick money turned her block into
a toll road

Anyone he'd introduce her block would soon seduce

But traffic wears down pavement so her price was soon reduced

To her late night binges her all night cringes

As her gutter over flowed with pipes and syringes

Lost and alone in despair's dark valley

Condemned and abandoned not even crime would walk her alley

Green lights became confused with yellow and red through
blurred vision

As she raced full speed ahead into a cul-de-sac collision

Of one way out and one way in

But without rules, speed limits and caution it all DEAD ENDS

Addiction

The first time should have let me know that you were far more than I could ever handle. But you felt so good and I blamed it on just that. It being my first time and all you had an unfair advantage. I mean you caught me off guard because I didn't know what to expect. Yeah I know you warned me, even told me to expect the unexpected but who wouldn't have been caught off guard by your feel and the uninhibited pleasures of satisfaction. So once more let me share the divinity of your essence. "Oh yeah that's it, just like that." It's amazing how the flavor of your sensuality warps the reality of the average man but not me. You see I can handle your passion. As a matter of fact I only come back because I know you need me in the same manner that I need you. You need me to make you feel complete and I need you to release stress. So come here and let me escape the same old same old for just a while and I'll make you feel like all you can and want to be. "Yeah that's my girl give it to me like you owe me something." Well I can eat later for now I'll be satisfied completely by the love that is you. You do love me don't you? I mean the same way that I love you. "A problem?" Listen to me the only problem is that there aren't enough hours in the day to spend with you. I'll always come back to you the one hundred percent pure sweetness of the guiding light to a lost soul in denial.

Forbidden Fruit of the Ghetto

We bloomed from the branches of poverty stricken misfortune

Happy to escape the withered vines of abortion

Seeds of societies burden bearers and oppressed

Harvested on hand me downs and what they had left

Every day is struggle every second's a hustle

Our leaves don't blow in the wind that's the movement of tussles

Searching for light, chasing opportunity

Praying that misfortune is not pursuing me

So many of my peers were plucked before they were ripe

Out of time before time could reveal what's right

Fallen to the streets addicted to currency

Society calling for their sweets conflicted by the urgency

To make money off us, bid to the highest made money offers

We live in the grassless jungles of obscurity where nobody

bothers

To take the time to smell the flowers

They figure why smell that stench you see that pleasure is ours

I've seen cherry stained streets from those who've called it quits

Tired of living life stressed out in the pits

Of obscurity, unsure of the, misery that awaits

Exchanging life for death hoping to change gates

To heaven from hell to freedom from jail

Searching for an oasis of opportunity from the ghetto's cold cells

Left out we can't elope with the mainstream

Sugar plumed hopes and thoughts of the same dreams

To rise above it all and provide security for our seeds

So that they may thrive in a garden that's cultivated without
weeds

Hero

May I be your hero, racing towards you in a bronzed chariot, wearing the breastplate of righteousness. For all I want to be is right by you. My feet shod with the gospel, every step I take drawing us nearer to a love blessed, conceived in the most high. I mean every queen needs a hero. Not that you need be saved, however may I. Will you allow me to bare some of your burden, my head dawning the helmet of salvation, in my right hand a sword which is the word of truth, which would grant me the wisdom and means to protect you from all that would attack your Queendom. In my left hand a rose, to remind me of your beauty and that you always need to be cherished and nurtured with the waters of love. May I accompany you through the sands of affliction and adversity, on to and oasis of comfort, a paradise where we can dine on black seedless grapes. May I be your hero?

Unscripted

Loving at the speed of light

Two souls racing at an unfamiliar pace

Traveling down a four lane highway using every one

Not really knowing which direction to go

No seat belts and no brakes full speed ahead

To a destination unknown yet so comforting

Holding on through potholes

Accelerating through hairpin turns

Hoping to find one another still there

When the road becomes straight

The speed limit to our happiness… unscripted

The laws of our fantasies and desires…unscripted

The road map to our love…unscripted

Sharing this love to the beat of life

Dancing hand in hand, cheek to cheek

Across an empty sheet of music

Leaving the trail of lovers footsteps

Drumming out a rhythm of

Sometimes it's better that it hurts

Contradicting snare claps of good and bad times

Often makes it worth the screams of the hi-hat

Through argument of ever changing tempos

But loves crescendo of work it out will overcome all

Creating a melody of bliss

The notes to which we move…unscripted

The words to our loves melody…unscripted

The theme song of our love…unscripted

Desert Flower

Confusing illusions of what I'm really pursuing

Perhaps my fantasies of you and I are merely a mirage

Nothing more than a collage

Of broke hopes and dream

We've both stood in love and were scorched by the heat of love

lost

I find reassurance in you my desert flower

Something more than a cactus a pillar of strength

A sign that love can endure beyond all trials and tribulations

To the true meaning of commitment

When my lips became parched from a lack of affection

I find the nurturing love I need deeply rooted in the waters of you

When I'm pricked by the needles of shallowness

It makes me appreciate the inner beauty of you

And realize anything worth having

Is worth sacrificing and working for

So my love my flower I walk through this desert of despair

Loneliness and heartache

Searching for you

My sun kissed dream.

Closer to My Dreams

Troubled beginnings, humbled endings in between a life of
sinning

So Much stress on my mind they've got my eyebrows thinning

Hair receding, heart beating twice the pace of the average

Hopes and dreams of better things a life of living lavish

Soul searching; the man in the mirror is a stranger

Captivated by danger constipated with anger

The rebirth of a broken man God please hold my hand

Walking through troubled times 4 footprints in the sand

And the sands of my hour glass past to fast

When you're addicted to hustling, sinning, and cash

I stand fast holding on to what's left

Trials tribulations I'm feeling so stressed

Violent scenes, sirens screams, it seems I'm losing faith

On the corner of destruction and pain which road do I take

Where does it lead? What do I need? Have mercy on my seed

It's not as bad as it seems just bring me closer to my dreams

Exodus to Genesis my underlying theme

To escape to new beginnings a never dying dream

Trying things I haven't seen hoped dreamed or fathomed

Opportunities to do things I couldn't imagine

Firmly grabbing every wish,

Ghetto bliss,

Mr. President and Pope

Give back the hope

Set the world free

Stop the bombing spree

Promise me this I'd lay down my own life

Bless my seed to succeed no more stress on my wife

Living life, without any boundaries

It never stops astounding me

How cold and unforgiving this blue balloon can be

Soon to see… Armageddon; are we forgetting?

Everything here is temporary so why are we bullshitting

I'm not shitting on the world, just gripping on a pearl

Placed firmly on my back while I stand and twirl

Anticipations got me waiting, feeling like a fiend

I'm so anxious I can't take it bring me closer to my dreams

Blind faith eyes closed trying to see what I believe

Clinched fists deep breath dying to retrieve

My thoughts of you last night's dream tomorrows fantasy

Today's an illusion tell me can it really be

Peppermint scented heaven in the arms of a felon

A natural born sinner makes love to angel now I'm jealous

Of myself I'm held in contempt

Don't judge me too strongly I'm trying to get a grip

Palms sweating, heart racing, stomach filled with butterflies

Tossing turning yearning for your sultry sighs

Mystified, spellbound, captivated and immersed

In the depths of you I'm diving head first

Infatuation, lust?

More like companionship and trust

Let me chase away your fears we can do a little something-
something

Loving through the early morning building blocks of love I'm
knowing

Sweating tossing to and fro and

Anticipations got me waiting feeling like a fiend

I'm so anxious I can't take it bring me closer to my dreams

Vision a late night scene my top down because it's clear skies

No bellowed rapes, yellow tapes, no one here dies

Lies, untruths, hollow slugs, bullet proofs

Three strikes, fiends hyped or drive by's out the coupe

Just the high speed chase of youth's that's chasing dreams

Adult's that chasing cream, elders chasing memories, so it seems:

A painting of perfection because I've spotted

No need for jail cells simply get it how you got it

Shot callers are scholars, big ballers are politicians

Attorneys, Masons, chemists, Lakers, Raiders and Physicians

We all wishing on a star praying to Jesus

We can make it happen it seems nobody believes us

Head bowed eyes closed as humble as it seems

Lord I turn to you to bring me closer to my dreams

Fabric of your life

Iron Clad walls

Hearts soft as cotton

Poorly knitted understanding

Started the shots popping

Polyester trigger fingers

Twitched with itchy reflex

Misunderstanding became misconstrued

And stretched beyond the capacity of latex

As prides of Teflon were stepped on

They released the first shots

But who fired and for what reason

They really knew not

Blue, red, purple, orange, brown California shades

Paisley bandanas hung from pockets in every array

Representing what they stood and fell for

Crips, Bloods, Grapes, Hoovers and Essays

On a larger scale

Much the same but sadly true

50 stars and satin stripes

Parading Red, White, and Blue

Armies of trained assassins

In blended camouflage fatigues

Whose mission is to shoot on sight

Blend in and deceive

Or a garment of perfection

Silk woven of truth

Raining sin ailing skin

Aiding friend and bullet proof

A way out of no way

All found in Christ

Cotton, polyester, satin or silk

What will be the fabric of your life?

Black Licorice

Your strut your stroll sophisticatedly grown

The way your hips sway screams sex appeal

Independently sexy the way you get it on your own

I could only imagine the way your touch would feel

I hate to admit it but damn I love your flavor

Addicted to the perfection of your body's curves and twists

Verbal stimulation your words I suckle and savor

Assata Shakur meets Me'Lisa Barber you're the perfect mix

Bitter to most but they don't understand

The ghetto's cold garden is where you were weaned

Your sweetness extends to every woman and man

At first sight everything's not always what it seems

Your roots deeply rooted in family and friends

A nurturing provider amongst other things

Conscious of self but not self-conscious ignoring those trends

That degrades the woman that is Queen to all Kings

Lost in the Translation

I meant to say I love you but something was lost in the translation from my brain to tongue. So what you probably heard was hey Ms. how are you? What's been up with you?

I wanted to caress your satin skin smoothly from head to toe. However something was lost in the translation from my fingertips to your hips. So what you felt was something more of an erotic sultry stroke of palm to chest for one sensual moment.

My heart wanted to scream to you. You and I in love eternal forever and always, but between beats pride stepped in and a rhythmic pulse of lets be friends resounding echoes drowned my hearts contractions for eternal companionship.

My arms yearned to embrace you passionately, the warmth of your subtle seduction next to me. However from shoulder to hand and from man to woman something was lost in the translation and what you got was probably nothing more than a hand shake a mere cordial greeting.

My lips even still are compelled to utter the words of ethereal thoughts consummating intimacies gently in your ear. But perhaps from cheek to cheek something dissipated in the translation and what was said was we're alone what's up.

Don't let the translation from my pen to pad to your eyes be misread and hearts misled understand I love you.

Don't let the translation from my thoughts to lips to your ears be misheard understand that I'll always be there

Don't let the translation from Spanish to French to English be misconstrued know that in every way possible what I hold for you is a love that's universal.

Missing in Satisfaction

Complicated patience through inexplicable absence of your

presence

I see you, I hear you, and we stand face to face together

In a separation known as alone

But I haven't moved one step where have you gone?

Visual confirmation, yes I know you are there

But where exactly is there?

Uncircumnavigated courses of your essence

I see the celestial light of your smile

But there are portions of your constellation that I don't recognize

Sequestered insecurities that securely guaranteed the promise of

our demise

How dare I ask that you give up security for a chance at a

Russian Roulette Love, leading to chalk lined silhouettes and hugs

If I bite the bullet again would even try to resuscitate us

Bulletproof promises abandoned on battlefields of forgotten

pleasure

Where mines amputate the legs of let's try this again

How can I run to you?

When you have run from me at every opportunity

Or maybe I was simply pursuing

High noon's' shadow of a love that you really shared with

someone else

And I was the delusional derelict on the laughing end of a joke

Whose butt was my heart

Heartache is a shitty smelling laughing gas

Choked out by fumes of solitaire

Excuse me for moving on

Temporary fantasies of pleasure

Cant out last the reality of pain incarnate

The embodiment of this is something I can't afford to turn back to

The emotional bondage of a debt that's unequally yoked to

a phantom lover

Morris Gamble

Keep Me From You

We are kin to the treasures of Egypt, Babylon, Zulu and Shabazz

We're the lost tribes of projects, Burroughs, wards, hoods and
ave's

Where the skies rain steel slugs

Creating puddles that deal drugs

Here amidst the tyrants and sirens, hustlers, brutes and the
violence

I feel worried through the temporary moments of silence

I walk with you in mind knowing none can harm me

As I trample through the tribes of gutters, sewers and zombies

Sporting chains with diamond studded misfortune

Medallions stained with the abortion

Of self enlightenment, pure righteousness, lost and misguided
with

Blunt in hand thinking they're as high as high can get

They sit on a picket fence and hustle for change

We used to sit-in and pick it as we hustled for change

No longer shackled by chains

But now we're shackled to chains

Broken glass and crack fiends

Hopeless dash through trashed scenes

Nothing's going to keep me from you

Chalked lines and road blocks

Lost minds who load Glock's

Nothing's going to keep me from you

From when the sun comes up until it's half past sleep

Let me be the reason that your passion slowly seeps

From your waist

With no waste

See it's more than the chase

Half of the pleasure is your subtle sweet taste

Compelling me to: touch you, tease you, lick you, please you

Hold you, free you, take time, and seize two

Moments just to stare at

Your body lying there at

Sexy angles as it glares back

Contemplating going bare back

Addicted to your mellow heat

Conflicted by the way we freak

The diction that our body speaks

Interpreted by satin sheets

Beads of sweat

The way you're wet

Subtle kisses on the neck

Excuse me Ms. but tell me if I'm incorrect

You like my strokes intensely deep

The liquid love of my tongues heat

To your clit's pulsing beat

As you passion starts to sleet

Drizzle rain

Pleasure pain

Some to give some to gain

In and out back and forth we exchange

Love taps

Butt slaps

Coincidence or perhaps

Your body was created to be my tongue's map

For buried treasure and nights of pleasure

Some may hope but they can't measure

Cravings for your touch

My body's yearning for your touch

Nothing's going to keep me from you

My addiction is your heat

Woman you make love complete

Nothing's going to keep me from you

The presence of a double fudged caramel beauty

With a nicely shaped plump apple bottomed beauty

Switching hips harder when she sees me

Sophisticated strut just to please me

Making eye contact that's more than the contact of eyes

The way she walks by just to brush her ass against my thighs

Suggestive invitations molesting innovations

Creating new ways just to touch my good vibrations

Just to let me know that she's with it if I'm with it

Told me she's got a description of pure pleasure and I fit it

Plus she's got a friend, light bright butter scotched obliged to
please

And they're the type of women that like to freak in threes

Make her man come back to back to back to back for more

Slurp him up, suck him off until he snores

Wake up to it, take him through it

If he's tired ride him ooh it

Sounds so good it reminds me of you

Makes me want to get home and spend time with you

Temptations of another's hips

Pleasure from some other lips

Nothing's going to keep me from you

The flirty batting of her eyes

The shapely thickness of her thighs

Nothing's going to keep me from you

Unfaithful

I'm not asking for forgiveness

Just taking a moment to relive this

Crazy situation

Now I'm not regretting that I did it

But damn... it was the business

But didn't compare to our love making

It's not about who's right or wrong

There was so much bullshit going on

Who would be the one to say

I was creeping you were cheating

Working late, business date every reason for deceiving

We both had games we'd play

Washing her love off my tip

But what's that I taste on your lip

It had me so confused

You know, I know those aren't my boxers

Black silk, I don't wear silk now it got ya'

That was just the first of clues

Her juices left my goatee soaked

I know we both smelled it in words we spoke

And now you say we need to talk

The way you approached me about confessions

Erotic stories of someone cheating sexing

And at the same time we complete the same thought

She and me, me and you, you and her

It was all a blink a blur

If only I had known

The way I liked her hips and waist

Was the same way you craved her pleasure's taste

We could have had some real freaking going on

Ms. Understood

She must have thought that I wanted to grope her behind

When actually I wanted to intrigue the pleasures of her mind

Maybe it was the Ms. Interpretation of me using the word lick

Not to be conveyed as tongue to hips but as me getting know you
being the shit

Now me sipping you slowly that's the learn the woman you are

Something I'd appreciate like an astronomer's study of the sky's
last star

I know they say men are from Mars and women are from Venus

So maybe that's why she Ms. Took my extension of hand as

extension of penis

I should have seen this, my words taken as obscene its

Happened before on maybe three or four occasions

How could Love's Angel be a sensual persuasion

To get you in bed when I see love as God's blessing

Perhaps that was lost in the translation from man to woman so

now I'm stressing

To find ways to put it bluntly or simply more stated

There's nothing X-tra Carricular, X-travagant,or X-ponentially

rated

About being addressed as an angel of love when it flows from my

pen

An extension of God's hand because all I write is manifested

through him

So please don't Ms. Understand me I meant no offense

I was simply asking how do I get to know you without the

awkwardness of introductions events

What it Tastes Like (part 1)

Your collarbone on my lips the sweetness of heavens bakery. Brown sugared truffles sprinkled with cinnamon delight. Enticing the return of my softly puckered lips to you, a mocha-latte caramel whip cream of pleasure. Slowly I'll run my tongue from shoulder to shoulder along your back. Stopping to enjoy the cotton candied pleasure of you neck, the gum drop nibbles of your ears. The slurps of you from breast to belly button to thighs an erotic carriage ride along a milk chocolate road of fantasy's delight. My tongues journey began on 36th street and C avenue in the Sugars Heights. Its slow descent along this chocolate road continued until it came to peanut butter circle where it paused to play in the recess of your belly button. On it proceeded beyond your hips to your thighway... Interstate Butter Pecan Bliss. The taste of your passion is that of a sensual factory producing introductions of dreams to reality. The warmth of my mouths reality now knows the dreamy sensuous heat of your womanhood. My taste buds become excited as they pair up and step to the rhythmically increasing throb of your clit between my lips as you release your intoxicating vanilla swiss almond Haagen Dazs nectar.

Taurean Queen

Bullish, seductive

Erotic, compulsive

Buck me if you must

Stubborn and driven

Compelling, fulfilling

Let me ride the thrusts

Of your ups and downs, short intrigues

Constant visions, lifelong dreams

How can I be the red flag in the eyes of a Taurean Queen

Ms. mellow, sexy, real

Enthralling yet concealed

My hearts main event

Caramel, cinnamon hope

I'm twirling but I know

You're only lassoed with your consent

With your permission may I have the pleasure

To learn to nurture, cherish, satisfy and treasure

The heart and desires of a Taurean Queen

Nneka

Now some may dream of a perfect 10 but not I. I dream of a five foot six perfect six. A chocolate coated oasis to my minds weary state, yet there you stand so much more than a dream. The reality of my hearts affection your eyes the shade of an ebony onyx pearl leading to your soul. Your stance is a whisper of sophistication seductively enchanting my minds state of self control with an open invitation to get closer to you. How could I not give in to heaven's addiction? Let me explain heavens addiction. It's the beauty of two things that complement one another, one completing the other to perfection. Some may say butterflies to gardens or air to lungs. In this case I'll say chemistry to biology. Although one may exist without the other it needs the other to complete it. Simply stated you bring my science of love to life transforming something stagnant into a breathing pulsing moving reality. Six beats of my heart creating one tone of adornment of the queen of my soul. Now how did I become fortunate enough to find my way to you? Surely it had to be the miracle we commonly refer to as divine intervention. The beauty of you divinely intervening with the key to my heart.

Selfish Lover

They say that what you have is gone before you really appreciate
it

However anyone's who's been in love knows the feelings are
undeviating

So he decided to take a chance on an openly hidden romance

Besides things like this didn't occur through mere circumstance

Never thinking circumstance may have picked him to be its next
victim

Looking back on what he had hoping and wishing

That he didn't give in to the temptation of lust

Without a second thought about her he was caught on the cusp

Of cheating, misleading in every way he'd be deceiving

His true love, himself and this woman this evening

But selfishly he fell into lusts grip the way he admired her hips

For so long, too long he desired her sips

Of another woman's nectar, yes his girl was his treasure

But it seemed to him he'd been with her forever

Caught in the same old same old everyday monotony

And to him the situation had really gotten to be

One he was in because of the comfort of knowing

The familiarity of love and no longer how they were growing

Together forever but more so apart

And was really staying with her not to break her heart

Selflessly selfish but he couldn't help it

Caught between loving and leaving and lust had compelled it

Sixty Blocks

I was born on the corner of poverty and struggle in a one room
shack

Fortunately breech birth I hit the streets running and I've never
looked back

Searching for better times in a better place

For the next four blocks I had to race

The cops sirens, hunger for violence, and everyday traps

Innocently guilty of walking while black

I was never pampered and don't shit where I lay

I hustle by night and make moves by day

Light struggles and heavy burdens have me growing up fast

6 blocks with the weight of the world on my shoulders a breather
At–Las

When I came to MLK Boulevard a temporary moment of peace

But broken dreams hopeless ambitions and false promise stood
across the streets

My progress was stopped by red lights and I'm waiting my turn

My rights are all wrong with each revolution a lesson is learned

3 blocks of passion with no direction full speed ahead moving
slow

4 left turns have me back where I was an entire revolution ago

2 blocks of hood rats that I wouldn't even approach

Claiming to be first class but their bags were all coach

6 blocks spent wondering why nobody likes me

Envy in their eyes as they stare at the chosen one unlikely

To make it through the next 7 blocks of prostitutes, playas
hoodlums and thieves

But I was weaned on hard times, adversity and government
cheese

So 4 blocks of bullshit, manure and drama couldn't turn my
stomach

But 1 intersection of my people turning their backs on one
another made me vomit

4 blocks of crack fiends and hustlers in a high speed chase

Pursuing false highs, hot rides and Mr. big face

3 blocks of struggles tears, for 2 more I cried softly

As I trampled through yellow tape and chalk lined young bodies

2 blocks of pick it signs protestors and community service

Falling on the deaf ears of elected government workers

10 blocks of self sacrifice spent on the grind

Trying to uplift my people and bring them all peace of mind.

Street's Wishing Well

A penny for my thoughts, rippled waters street blocks

From my footsteps dodging hollow point raindrops

Hood hopes are hustle hard with hints of humbled hearts

Hop scotching through terrains of troubled times and pool sharks

New starts same endings so we're caught in a loop

Of constant struggle, hood hustles, johns, pimps, prostitutes

Broken glass gavels smash for the stuff that they do

Seven years up state wishing for you

Freedom and good fortunes my dollars in bigger portions

We rolling in drop top Porsches my dimes are all horses

Thoroughbred no ponies they all stallions

I'm down with Michael Vick but watch out for Foul Cons

Back stabbers false friend's chumps and stool pigeons

Home chilling while his man is stuck on a sentence

Visions of progress the streets are heartless

Life in the hoods like creased khaki's hot lined and hard pressed

A nickel kiss of luck, tongue kissing sin we fucked; eyes closed
blind faith it seems we're lost in the game

Poverty's laceration's, robberies scars still chaffing, the bandages
are diamond chains to show we are flossing the pain

Of hard times, ill fates, broken dreams, false promise

When it really comes down to I guess that I'm as

Guilty as it gets I'm balling with nineteen cents

Nine on one side a dime on the opposite

One loaded cocked to spit, the other holding my cock and sips

Addicted to whips, making major moves and chips

I flip pounds on the low down like Dominique Dawes

Leaving epileptic cops the way I'm shaking the law

No flaws no seizures, the hoods Rome and I'm Caesar

A natural born leader guaranteed to be the

Soul, light and truth, the street divinity

Comfort, guide, protector the hoods holy trinity

A dime to feel love is the grind to real thugs

The block to prostitutes a Glock to steel slugs

Hand in hand, cheek to cheek, companionship to a freak

My words over beats, a hustler to the streets

Inseparable conceptual marriage in true style

With rules regulations pre nups unwritten vows

Eyes closed blind faith, staring down temptation

I could vision her face

Her eyes shine true diamond rare cut gems

And when her head and lips stop her tongue still spins

The Benz bubble eye and since money ain't a thing

I'm going to scoop Crenshaw put some diamonds on her ring

And I might wife Florence, Sunset or maybe Vine

I'm going to finger fuck Main, let Central hold my nine

Spend time in Hawthorne, blow a little Doty

You see I'm married to the streets and everybody knows she

From south central my broad mad hood

Long beach, Watts, Carson, Compton, Inglewood

Together

I know I haven't known you long but you remind me of the golden days of Babylon. Revered for its beauty strength and admired by all. I would be your king Solomon and you my queen Sheba. One together in the blessings of God promised and everlasting love with its foundations deeply rooted in the most high. Faith in you, in us, in him.

Although we may choke on the bread of adversity and be bathed in the waters of affliction we will endure and overcome together. Every diamond must go through the pressures and tribulations of compression, through the trials of time and change. A change in which we could grow…Separately, individually together as one. The difference in time, the difference in age doesn't matter. Eyes closed, heart open, mind blown I realized there is no difference. No difference in love, in faith, nor in you and I. so from hence forth I'll hope that you will allow me to nurture the maple brown sugared licorice roots of you that extend from the heavens to the soils of my soul forever.

Black Sunshine

The early morning hue of your butter scotched rise

Brings a smile to my face when I open my eyes

What better way to start my days

Than the gentle touch of your warming rays

The perfect complement to the early morning's dew

The aftermath of a night of loving shared between me and you

I was afraid to love but you warmed me up to the idea

Helped me lose my inhibitions with actions so sincere

You're high noon's caramel toned affection a perfect elu of
sophisticated grace

Moving my desires to a whole new direction but I'm up for the
chase

Of something hot and heavy long and steady, pursuits of love's
dream

God's blessing to a man something more than a Queen

Perfection at its peak let's say a Nubian Goddess

A combination of Mmm good and lord have mercy yet I'm still
being modest

Understand my goal is to please you I'm not afraid of working up
a sweat

How is it that you keep me hot and bothered with just a kiss on
the neck

Ms. Twilight Sunset a red boned addiction that has me thoroughly
amazed

In awe and captivated by your enchanting ways

Love has me following you so if that's where you really want to
reside

I'll find the perfect place for us to settle down on the west side

Where we can grow to learn one another's ways in love

And you be my peace of mind metaphorically my thoughts of a
dove

Yet so much more at least in any event

My light house guiding me to love my backbone my pillar of

strength

I'll always be mesmerized by the glow of your midnight ebony
seduction

In the pitch black of night I can feel your warmth you've got me
clutching

At love with blind faith, 20/20 vision of me remaining by your
side

Blindly trusting love's perfect sight to be our tour guide

Through times as explosive as radioactive nitroglycerin

Tell me what's heavy on your mind and heart I promise I'm
listening

I know that God's love descends on me through interpretations of
your rays

I'll rest in homage of him 52 times but pursue you endlessly for
313 days

Close

Hand in hand we exchange eye contact. Intrigued I gazed harder hoping that I could fall in to those ebony pearls that lead to your soul. May I, is it possible that we can become close? Cheek to cheek I whispered into your ear "Drawn from the wells of grace, poured from the flasks of sophistication and dipped in the nectar of beauty" woman you are all that I dreamed of and more, so much more. Do you desire, would you allow us to become close? So near so close that the moon would blush, our emotions so tight that the oceans would hush and listen to the sounds of us. Chest to breasts we align our bodies like the heavenly deities of a solar eclipse. Passionately I try to move even closer, closer to caressing the taste buds of your mind. Can we, how about us becoming close?

What Can Be Better

The ocean is relevant again

Because I'm floating on thoughts of you

Relaxing current of bliss keep me focused

On the now, but somehow

I always drift back to thoughts of our last encounter

The gravity of pleasure lifts me to the tropic of Orion

What can be better than this: Bare chest to back we stare down at the stars

What can be better than this: Cerebral cortex conscious dream of a love like ours

Angels are heaven sent again

Because the most high has blessed me with you

Honestly you're my favorite non-fiction

Queen first born-third sent to demonstrate love

Its affect uplifting civilizations, resurrecting hope sparking revolution

Through reevaluation of re-evolving

Constantly allowing me third born planet to firstly revolve around you

What can be better than this: Being the chosen love of the love chosen by the most high

What can be better than this: Simply stated you and I.

Biko

Beautiful Stranger

When I first spoke to you I knew that love had found me

One mere verbal exchange and I had learned to love profoundly

Your words said so much yet meant so much more

I'd finally come to understand the true meaning of the word
adore

Our souls met on the infinite plane of introductions

Our minds rendezvoused at the thought of this leading to
something

From the first extension of your beautiful hand

I knew I wanted to become a better man

So right from the beginning I was conspiring it's true

Intently pensively contemplating on ways of aspiring to be the
right man for you

Our hears on a journey far beyond the seduction of lips, bosom
and thighs

One mention of your name coincided with tears of joy in my eyes

Our passions frolic on the coast of righteous delight

Silhouettes completing one another to perfection without a
sunrise in sight

Your touch all too familiar your voice resembled a tone

That accelerated the beats of my heart and that my desires had
already known

Where I knew you from maybe a past life's love or that of an
alternate dimension

All that really mattered was us getting closer and finding the
perfect position

For enjoying one another's conversation, quick wit, stimulating
tidbits

And how we can be all alone in this crowded room of misguided
misfits

In between my dreams is the heavenly sensation of a reality that is
you

Surrounding my reality is the dream of us hand in hand walking
on water pursuing a love that's true

There you are a constant vision of where I need to be

And although I've never met you I'd spend a lifetime trying to see

The grace of your stroll the perfection of your diction

The reality of your dreams of righteous upliftment

The first time I see you this love will grow stronger so I'm patiently waiting

Hoping that sometime between now and eternity I get to

show my appreciation

The Hands of Time

Immersed in sins envy, Birthed at 6:20, the hands of time showed the signs six to four odds against me. Weaned on the breast of affliction, chasing money an addiction, lip locked with hard times I hustle with conviction, living in nonfiction. Reality is a hard pill to swallow, I hustle hard every day the only day off is tomorrow, beg borrow and steal, you don't know how it feels. To sleep outside waking up at 7:11, an uphill battle surrounded by 1 to 3 killers and 6 to 8 felons. Coppers slowly trailing... every move I make, every friend I dap, and every woman that I fuck every phone is tapped. 9:45 shook left to change the game, my friends batteries stopped clock froze he should have done the same. 0:00 hundred hours, emotions showered and a tear drop falls, another soldier has crossed over and was lost to the cause. Living without laws the sands of time reverse, my life a loop of constant struggles and it seems my curse, 12:30 to 2:20 second to none in my stressing, carrying the cross for all my people something more than a blessing.

1:00 honey was hot so tight just nineteen, college bound knowledge hound daddy's girl ebony queen.

Boarding school, ignoring fools but found love at 3, because he applied the right approach plus the right degree. Slight envy because it's what all men seek, together watching father time change the moon to sun on the beach. Educated her on body language something she did not know, his palms caressed her hour glass figure and made her sands just flow. 7:05 blessed with child but still an uphill struggle, motherhood, work and school a hard act to juggle. Befuddled and overwhelmed but persevered to succeed, graduated infatuated with raising her seed.

Started this journal so I could learn you on this game called life, the hands of time has touched us all some with stress and strife. 6:30 yeah I've fallen but I always rose, fallen again got back up shit at times I dove. Ducking bullets and bullshit all that comes my way, praying to God for 12:30 knowing he can lead me straight. Into the gardens of Eden away from all the drama and stress, crashing in the game of life but still driven so I know I'm blessed, with a confidant, a shoulder, lover and supporter, won't meet him face to face until I'm gone but I met her at a quarter past five, won't dispute, so acute with her dress thoughts and tone, love me for rich or poor, better or worse so I'm never alone. My house now a home she steps away when I'm faking, keeps an eye out for me and prays that I make it. See I'm a man on my own but she makes me complete, love triangle we're the base and Gods the peak. So trials and tribulations I'm defeating all test, I thank God for sending me his representative right here in the flesh.

Al-Freeda Moor

ALINA: In every aspect of the word, your diction, your stroll the way you move beyond the common transcending thoughts of love by expressing a nurturing care for those whom haven't even realized their own capabilities of love or their capacity for them. Missed opportunities pursuing trivial things left us in a state of flux, however being in your presence allowed me to see a Noble character through the blessing of your grace.

Freeda: A magical consultation with the divinity of an oracle. How did I not realize that your words, your emotions, your state of devotion were based in something higher than both of us. A divine blessing speaking truth and good fortune opening the eyes of a blind lover whose ears were poorly tuned, yet your direction and frequent affection redirected the common sense of a weary traveler to a frequency of self realization. To put it bluntly you freed a mind that was shackled by the dreams of others and the bounds and limits of their capabilities.

Moor: Surely a beauty who has traversed the seas of my heart. Deriving from the word NUR the light of love and the love of light, walk with me as you once allowed me to walk with you in a young love that matured to a mutual respect and understanding of exactly what love is. Some say that less is more, well I will always truly believe in the depths of my heart that someone I can "Call-Lean" on will always be More.

1991-Eternity

PLEASURE

Stimulation

My heartbeat quickened to the pace of a sewing machines needle and my temperature rose as she slid off her thong down her thighs past her perfectly manicured toes to their final resting place on the freshly waxed hard wood floor. Her body's movements sashayed to the rhythm of seduction over to the bed as she pulled back the covers and sprawled across the sheets. It was at that moment I came to know the true meaning of the word lust. My lips began to lust the hazel nut complexioned milky feel of her thighs and my sexualities hunger growled in anticipation of dining on her flavors of passion. Her beauty was all natural no additives needed she had sexiness covered from every angle. Her breasts soft and round provoking arousal, her eyes a mesmerizing delicacy inviting me to get to know her passion, her ass the perfection of a ripe plum; firmly soft, round, plump and so sweet. Her hips best described as fascinatingly kissable, a delectable cuisine of chocolate covered strawberries water falling into her thighs. Damn her thighs! A sprinters envy, a models dream, a curvaceous playground for my tongue to slide up and down, sway back and forth until I finally reached her moist box.

There she laid across my sheets like an evenly spread thick

scoop of creamy peanut butter glazed with caramel addiction, craving the grasp of my hands on her hips, yearning for the caress of my tongue, screaming for the deeply intense strokes of my manhood from every freakish angle. Butterflies of anxiety became the flaps of an eagle pounding inside my stomach. Never before was I so anxious to touch, feel, and please anyone in my life. After several deep breaths I moved closer and closer until our bodies became one warm chocolate formation of pleasure. I could feel the beads of sweat race across my back, roll off my shoulders and splash on to her thighs, which I had pinned over my shoulders creating a pool of passion warmth and moisture. Yet it still fell short in comparison to the passion warmth and moisture of her river. Her river was a warm steamy paradise of flowing titillating excitement. With every up stroke the current of her sensuality pulled me back in as she squeezed her walls tightly guiding me in. The warmth of that reentry was an atmosphere of plush security. Letting me know that everything was going to be ok her babbling brook whispered to my desire to please her, softly telling me how she thoroughly enjoyed everything that I was doing. The way her stomach convulsed when I stroked from left to right, how her thighs trembled when I slid all of me in from tip to base filling her and from the reaction of her sighs, lips quivering and walls palpating I could tell that she was feeling me as well.

Our sensations of pleasure only limited by the night turning to morning so let's take advantage of the moment and continue riding the suns early rays to the height of orgasmic delight. I know you've climaxed once but let me take you on an erotic venture into the safari of light headedness, body numbness, head changes and body shivers as we hunt the pinnacle of touching, teasing, caressing and stroking known as orgasm again and again. Your sighs mighty clouds of joy raining soprano toned raindrops of satisfaction all over me until I become drenched. However I won't stop until you're hoarse from late night screams of "ooh daddy just like that, keep it right there, you are all over my spot."

Arousal

Imagine the pleasure of you sitting on my face

Until the secretions of your passion are written on my face

Scribbled amidst the flicks of my tongue

Dribble betwixt the tricks of my tongue's

Encounter with thighs, clit, lips and excitement

Empowering your sighs, moans and screams of excitement

To rain freely and crash against windows at my tongue's request

As my oral skills succumb to your hips grinds and passions
requests

To slurp harder, go deeper, intense with no slack

To lurk further, flow steeper, become taught with no slack

To its circling, winding wall to wall motions

Tidal waving, shore crashing receding type motions

Contrasted by the gentle cooling winds pulled between my lips

As clit sits firmly erect between my lips

Nibbled gently, stroked discreetly, so you'll convulse between my
lips

If you're with me, please don't cheat me, go ahead and convulse

between my lips

In uncontrollable body numbing chill vending shivers

Soul portable partially mumbling will bending shivers

From which you might come down but never return

And every time you hear my name you'll quickly return

To that feeling of pleasure

Always and forever feeling my pleasure

Body Kiss

The meeting of lips, our passionate greeting is this

Subtly intoxicating grip, a sensual body kiss

We stand chest to breast, embraced in desire

Sending passion on a quest, to find true love and conspire

On ways to keep us enchanted, beyond the meeting of eyes

Let's not take this moment for granted, as I slide my hand from
your waist to thighs

Drawing our bodies closer, to arousals cusp

For so long I've wanted to know the, feel of your touch

The gentle nibble of your neck, as you close your eyes

As my tongue scribbles out let's, chase passion's sighs

Until we've found, what your body's been craving

As your heartbeat pounds, against my tongue and its saying

"Slowly mold me, with your slurps

Passionately hold me, until it hurts

So good that I shiver," embraced for impact

My passion begins to quiver, and softly whispers back

"Give in to my stroke, and gently wind it back

Let what's moist become soaked, as your body contracts

Tightens-releases gently squeezes, to my penetration

Faint of breath you can barely breathe, from my sweet sensations

Of in out up and down, I can feel your body cringe

Sighs and moans are the sounds, as I take you on a pleasure binge

Convulsion

Walked in the door dropped my coat and inhibitions

Thoughts of our bodies' contortions in every freak position

Ran through my mind my tongue down your spine

Proceeded by greetings and a freakish bump and grind

Followed by the sensual chase of my hands to your waist

As my tongue become familiar with your chocolate honey dew

taste

Your body's erotic slurps is what my lips have been craving

Lips to lips enjoying every drip I sip your nectars intoxicating

Shimmy, shake, quiver, erotic expulsion

Let me bring you to the ultimate convulsion

Is it the way that you're riding it… that's got me biting lips

Or pleasures warmth when I'm inside of it…that sends my mind

adrift

I can't pin point exactly what it is but woman your enticing fits

Slowly you're taking me to the edge of passions cliff

And I'm ready to jump into your chocolate oceans bliss

Maybe it's the way your walls are grasping me that makes my

body tremble

Perhaps it's the gentle whispers of your body asking me to

freakishly give it to you

In manners akin to pleasure fantasy and lust

As they grab pen and pad and take notes from us

While you entice my coconut rain propulsion

Woman you are to me the ultimate convulsion

After glow

Body's tingle

We softly mingle

Between the sheets

Pleasure meets

Friendly giggles

Erotic tickles

Beads of sweat

That led to sex

Drench the pillow

Moonlight outlines you Silho…Uette

Still wet

Subtle kisses on the neck

Chills across your body bookmark the trek

Of erotic slurps, that quenches the thirst

Of the parched throats of passion to see who cums first

Natural highs' endorphins released

Pleasures endorsed morphine for sleep

Body heavy mind light and I know you're feeling like

You don't want the morning to interrupt the night

Canvas of Love

Her body was the art of love's dream,

The perfect shade of beauty untouched and so clean

Awaiting the strokes of the right paintbrush and colors

Only to be caressed by the most choosy of lovers

Her thighs two pillars of caramel fudge

Sculpted to perfection without fingerprint nor smudge

Erotically coated with two coats of my tongue down her spine

Her hair pressed as straight as it could get and pulled straight back

As I massaged her scalp and finger painted her hair jet black

As my tongue and her neck became intimate

I realized her skin was as soft as skin can get

Egyptian soft silk laced with a golden brown under tone

Rising with each sigh circling with each sensation

Coating her breast with a dark shade of stimulation

Deeper than blue a sultry undefined hue

Enticing the release of her ivory creamed dew

Now this might be inconsiderate but I teased it a little bit

Air brushing four different shades of pleasure from each thigh to clit

We stood locked lips to lips I could tell her favorite color was devotion

When I mixed honesty with sincerity and got a new shade of raw emotion

Her hips mumbled, called, screamed to me they yearned to be painted

Her eyes the color of a leather rawhide camel skin that's kind different now ain't it

Slightly glossed with arousal contrasted by the tones of affection

Adding my candy coated strokes of love meant perfection

Last Night's Dream

Woke up and the clock read 5:30 am. My heart racing, forehead misty and a bead of sweat sat on my brow. Still slightly groggy I tried to sit up when I noticed the curvature of your back arched into a perfect capitol S. Your hands firmly grabbing the base of my manhood, your lips wrapped around the tip slowly gripping, grasping, clutching, and slurping up and down. Your ass high in the air bouncing jiggling to the rhythm of you mouth's motions. With mouth and hand moving in one synonymous motion, one coating with lust the other stroking encouraging busting you gazed deep into my eyes. Sensually you ran your tongue across my vein of pleasure circling the tip allowing me to regain my composure. As I caught my breath you reinserted me into your mouth. However this time it was different. The way you rotated your wrist in semicircular motions like a gymnast gracefully swirling across a pommel horse gripping and rewrapping as you ran your tongue and bottom lip around the head of my manhood. With each grope each stroke the convulsions of my thighs grew more intense. With both hands you grabbed me firmly. The strokes of your hands were twice as fast as that of your mouth enticing me to explode. Body quivering head spinning eyes heavy I fell into a deep slumber as I hear you chuckle "Yeah baby just like that."

Intermission

Panting tongues

Ranting lungs

Overheated exhausted from

The energy expelled, compelled by passions scrum

On playgrounds of satin sheets

Sex games between combating freaks

Take its toll on two bodies that can barely speak

Dare not move, dare not blink

Stare into each other's eyes and think

Is this real? This blissful feel

The sex appeal seems surreal

It's so good I can't conceal

These deep breaths...Ready yet?

Moments of pensive retrospect

Reveal that the last moment only fails in comparison to the next

Deep breath... almost ready, yes!

Move that there, let me grip this here

Just relax baby I'm going to steer

And take control as we change position

As we work our way through this intermission

Tomorrows Fantasy

Adjusting the shower head to a pulsating massage I turned around as the warmth of the water streamlined down my back my thoughts drifted to you and there I stood day dreaming of your sensual touch. You walked in the room frost bitten bottled water in one hand gracefully demanding desires attention. Placing the bottle on the counter next to the bed you leaned over and whispered in my ear "Get naked baby its massage time." As I laid face down on the bed she ran her fingers delicately from shoulder to shoulder. The tips of her fingers pulling stress from my muscles while the palm of her hand replacing it with relaxation. She stated "Let me know if it's too much" to which I replied "It can never be too much love just do you." At that moment I felt her grab the bottled water and take a sip. Without warning there was a spine chilling single drop of water on my shoulder zigzagging down my back this Jack Frost touched drop of water was met in the middle of my spine by the warmth of her tongue. She went back to softly knuckling my back transversely from hip to shoulder down my side and back up transversely from hip to shoulder when I felt one drop, two drops, three drops, pause, one drop, two drops sensually chilling my back. The ice cold water running down my spine was stimulatingly contradicted by the warmth of her womanhood being erotically rubbed back and forth across the small of my back. The chilled water met the warmth of her lips creating a sultry puddle of passion. She grasped both shoulders tightly as she began grinding harder, faster until she climaxed. Quickly she took another gulp of water and proceeded to slurp the pool of ecstasy she'd just created when the cold sprinkles of the showers brought me back to reality.

If Walls Could Speak (part.1)

His head buried in the depths of her passion, he arose briefly like a dolphin emerging for a breath of air and splash, right back into the fathoms of sensuality's ocean. Her passion rippled slowly in all directions upon his re-entry, slowly gaining momentum from his tongue swirling pearl stroking actions. Until her sighs tidal waved bouncing echoing back and forth off my sides. As he arose from his knees and said "Come here and join me in paradise" he stood her up and bent her over the edge of the bed, caressing her back with his palms gliding sensually hovering floating like a butterfly through a garden of chocolate dandelions. The soft flutters of his wings strokes moved her petals in the wind to the direction of goose bumps until he reached her hips where he landed. Grasping tightly he slid inside of her. Her head turned to the side, fists full of sheet, leg quivering reaction told the story of how she enjoyed that initial penetration. The joy on her face was that of a toddler tasting chocolate for the very first time craving another bite. Her insatiable moans of "Give it all to me daddy" encouraged his waist twisting angle stroking pounding; deeper, harder, more intensely, intently trying to bring her to orgasm. Gently he began to nibble on her shoulder, still grasping her waist while stroking intently. The biting of her lips soon replaced the subtle sighs as she grasped the sheets more tightly. He tossed his head back and stroked until they both climaxed.

As he walked to the restroom she rolled over on to her back. Stomach still convulsing involuntarily every time she exhaled; with long slow deep breaths she tried to bring her body back to reality form the celestial planes of orgasmic pleasure. Eyes closed she ran her hands from neck to breast, to stomach, to thighs as if to reassure herself everything was still in place and in one piece. When he walked in the room, kissed her softly on the neck then cheek as he laid beside her, she rolled over nestled her head on his chest and whispered "My body's so heavy, I mean heavily numb kind of light. It's like I can't feel it but… but it tingles all over with a warm sensation. Not warmth like fire but the warmth of the taste of cinnamon. Well I can't explain it." She wrapped her legs around his thighs and unknowingly began to grind her woman hood on him as she continued to mutter and mumble at conversation. "I'm still wet, damn near soaked and I can't control it or stop it. Actually I don't want to either." When he stood up with her in his arms her legs instinctively clamored to his waist as he inserted himself into her warmth. With each stroke they grew nearer to me until her satin skin became one with the top layers of my paint. Her sweat passionately coated my skin creating a layer of sensual erotica. With each insertion, withdrawal, insertion her body melted more oozing into the depths of me until it came to the point that one could no longer differentiate between her almond complexion and the off white of my own. For the first time I had become the wings of an angel. Her body being pressed against me was indeed a heavenly feeling. With a "Pop" created by the Suck-tion of the small of her back he tore her away from me. A quick dismount a 180 degree turn and they were back at it his palms spreading her ass cheeks, her palms embracing mine. The passion in the room so thick it began to fog the windows of my perception. His rhythm grew faster as she used me to support her back and forth ass bouncing. The arch in her back was that of a long bow being pulled taught to the limits of its elasticity. Indeed he was her archer pulling her tightly with each withdrawal repeatedly darting, piercing, and pounding her bull's-eye with each insertion. With one hand on her hip and the other on her shoulder his knees buckled as he fought for balance. Her juices splashed racing down his thighs as climax took control of the room.

Mind S.E.X.

I don't mind if you don't mind our minds meeting and engaging in S.E.X. Understand what I mean by sex is Stimulating Each X-rated fantasy that's ever crossed your mind. The verbal rhapsody of our conversation closing the door on inhibition and allowing us to become familiar with one another urging us to move closer to joy's ride of full speed ahead passion. Driving our souls to standing on the verge of testing our mental, physical, emotional and spiritual stamina while wondering if we could out last the honeymoon of ass grabs and giggles and test time with our early morning pillow talk following the pursuits of your fantasies.

Your fantasy of us in the shower and me becoming your water a warm sensation of relaxation coating your desires with the pleasures of seduction. Like water I'll conform to your shape fitting you, touching you, coating you, stroking you to perfection. Allow me to roll on over and off your satin skin taking you to the cusp of arousal. I'll glide down your body teasing your nipples to erection playfully circling your belly button. Slowly I'll move around to the small of your back down your shapely ass and thighs before becoming intimate with your lips. May I cleanse you of all your worries stress and troubles? May I be your oasis? A chocolate coated dream no longer a figment of your imagination but a vacation of tongue strokes, long strokes, warm oiled massaged, self-indulged, pampered paradise showing you the true meaning of the words liquid love.

Our fantasy of foreplay would be something like a game of kiss and tell. I'll run my tongue across you kissing, licking and nibbling at your caramel brushed honey glazed body as you release sighs of pleasure in the harmonious chord of "Damn just like that" telling me how much you like the warm sensation of my mouth intimately caressing your dreams detail with reality. The strokes of my tongue across your body a Novocain based hallucinogen killing you slowly bringing on head changes as you drift back and forth across the borders of reality and fantasy in a state of delusional bliss. Vision us out at sea, the sun peeping through the windows of our fantasies desires, the ocean rocking back and forth to my deep…Deep in and out strokes of you. Tell me how you like it I can tell that you're excited from the rise of your waters, the pleasure induced quiver of your stomach every time that I down stroke. Let's ride the waves of orgasm to shore.

Yes I do. I vow to make tonight one you'll never forget as we seal our vows of eternal companionship making the heavens blush on top of silk sheets and crushed rose petals, surrounded by Burberry scented candles lit with the passion of our consummation. Tonight will be one of many spent adoring you, admiring you, exploring you, satisfying you. Here I am adoring the essence of your woman hood admiring the depths of your strength character and beauty. Exploring the complexity of what drives you and motivates you, satisfying your need to be held loved and understood all the while loving making love to you. The feel of your lips upon mine is like a ride upon a marshmallow cloud to the doorstep of paradise. My hands on your hips, your arms around my shoulder an embrace of sensual affection, as we seduce climax into joining us, no offense but would you Mind S.E.X?

Deep Impact

Do you really want to do this? Understand once we get started there is no turning back from the stomach rippling, sheet drenching, pleasure sipping episodes that I create. Wait, hold up… I'm going to need you to read this and sign here and here and initial there. Yeah that's my standard contract releasing me from all liability for all thigh convulsing activity which may lead to ad*dick*tion. Now let me slide between your thighs and wrap your legs around my waist as I stroke until I see that look on your face. That one, right there I love the way it screams that the feeling of me is so intense that you can't take any more yet your body yearns for more, more of the feel of your waters cascading on the firmness of me, the intensity of my strokes enticing your warm coconut Niagara Falls to drench the sheets of my bed. Sit back relax and enjoy the moment as I take my time doing what it is that I enjoy doing more than anything else. Without a doubt that's pleasing you. I love being the fault line that runs so deep in your pleasures that your body shakes, quivers, earthquakes to the tempo of my long deep injections. Each of those moment X-ponentially increasing in pleasure. The feel of your heat, the freakish tugs of me pulling your hair, the way your walls grasp me upon down strokes re-entry, the way my tongue circles your nipples bringing them to erection as our bodies draw nearer to climax nothing short of perfection. Yes love that's it. Don't hold back. Allow those moans to become sighs and those sighs to become the screams to the heavens thanking the most high for the way I fill you completely, thrill you discreetly, hold you so cuddly, mold you like putty, encourage head changes, concur with sweat's rages of passions long convulsions, contractions love emotions brought on by my stroke! Just like that.

If Walls Could Speak Part 2

I'd been waiting for this for a while. His tongue thrust between my lips and with winding circular motions he caressed me from side to side with the tip of his tongue. The sensuous heat of his mouth was comparable to that of my own heat. Ninety – eight degrees and rising, rising to the temperature of the sun beaten desert ground on a smother hot summer day. Passions heat rose from his tongue making me delusional, weary and weak for the moment I could embrace his manhood and cradle it tightly. Gently rocking it up and down, back and forth until I put it to sleep. But this was no mirage it was the head on collision between stimulation and pleasure on the rail road tracks of climax. Erotically he teased me sliding his manhood from lips to clit to insertion and back until my waters rose to the edge of anxiety's pond and I screamed "Give me that, stroke me with that, let me have all of that please!" as he inserted the tip I released a small sample of nectars moisture…

Involuntary Convulsions Experience

I sat in the room anxiously anticipating the moment I could intervene between these two lovers. Now usually I patiently wait my turn, but pleasure had just taken over for arousal and he was doing the damn thing, their bodies contorting to positions only familiar to the grip of love and it was a picture of ecstasy finger painted by the God of Karma Sutra. As he inhaled I rode the scent of blackberry incense into her lungs. Infectious with desire taking my time I spread slowly from head to toe searching, waiting for a moment of weakness to make my move. Devilishly I teased, squeezing the walls of her womanhood briefly before making my escape back to her thighs before she could reach climax. On I made my way to the throbbing of her clit encouraging them to take a ride with me along the climax express. This would be a one way trip to the heights of orgasm with stops at the seldom frequented ports of light headedness and breath taken city. This high speed all night journey was the guaranteed conflict between how fast they could get to where they want to be and holding off to enjoy the sheer pleasure of the moment. When it was least expected I began to rise slowly in her stomach. Rocking back and forth from hip to hip, pausing, running laps inside her belly button streaming from stomach to thighs down to her toes. Slightly tingling, morphing between the sensation down her spine to the erotic tension in his shoulders…neither her slow deep breaths nor his highly focused concentration could hold me back. I seized control of the moment and was moving in for the kill. I ran through his body the same way I did hers. Traveling the overwhelmingly hot road of pleasure where his Boulevard of "Yeah take that!" intersected with her Avenue of "Give me that and make my rain come down." Bringing his level of excitement to a place he'd never experienced before until he lost control and savagely devoured her passion with intense strokes of sheer satisfaction. Grinning from ear to ear, pleased I stepped back to gaze upon the fruits of my labor. Their bodies laid motionless, minus the occasional quiver from the accidental brush of one another from the aftermath of a night with me. As I thought to myself "I.C.E. you are one COLD piece of work."

Is it Time To

Just because it's half past twelve

And I worked a double shift

Is it time to say good night

Only time can tell

Of what tonight's passion will consist

You know it's not time to say good night

Lights down low you're pulling back the sheets

Heading towards the pillow and the alarm is set

Is it time to say good night

You're the chocolate pudding I yearn to eat

Seductive sensual erotic glimpses of your silhouette

You know it's not time to say good night

I know you've climaxed twice

And your body is sensitive to touch

Is it time to say good night

Slurping your passion with my tongue and ice

Shivering shaking quivering quaking how you fiend for my
clutch

You know it's not time to say good night

Slowly the night becomes the dawn

And our bodies succumb to exhaustion

Is it time to say good night

Stroking with intentions of leaving your body numb

Groping grinding turning your river into an ocean

You know it's time to say good night

Keep it Right There

Keep the light on I want to see it all

From the petite frame of your waist to the shape of your lips when you call

My name in pleasure coincides with the convulsion from stomach to thighs

Your fists full of sheets, caramelized rain and multi toned sighs

My strokes got you using my name in vein like a heroin addict

I'm your freakish, under cover, forbidden, tasty habit

Compelling you to come back to back to back to back

I'm telling you, warning you make sure you want just that

It's the pleasure of addiction like lungs to air

Every time you breathe you'll be reminded of how I Keep it Right There

Right there intently… Keep it

Right there intensely… Keep it

Right there seclusively…Keep it

Right there exclusively… Keep it

Right there religiously… Keep it

The arch of your back the slope of your spine

The way you bounce it back your freakish slow grind

Your up and down riding the rhythm of your hips

The warmth of your moisture your walls gentle grips

Teasing me, squeezing me, groping me, grabbing me

Seductively, pleasing me, openly, having me

Contradicted in pleasure still holding back

As I give it all to you fighting off climax

Lost in your love none can compare

All I ask is that you Keep it Right There

Right there pleasing me… Keep it

Right there squeezing me...Keep it

Right there coating me...Keep it

Right there convulsing me...Keep it

Can I keep it right there in your spot?

Stroking your passion until your body becomes hot

Overheated with arousal from the inside out

As you bite your lips and your desire starts to shout

For my feel, my stroke, my clutch

My lips my tongue my hands my touch

Caressing your walls painting them with care

As your sighs scream to me Keep it Right There

Right there holding me...Keep it

Right there molding me...Keep it

Right there soaking me…Keep it

Right there stroking me…Keep it

Right there drilling me…Keep it

Right there filling me…Keep it

Librarian Woman

There she sat eyes batting glasses pulled down skirt pulled back showing her shapely caramel thighs one leg crossed over the other. I inquired "Ms. could you direct me to the romance section. She replied "Follow me." She led me upstairs to the far corner. All the time my eyes fixed on the card catalog of her hips, and the petite rotund seduction of her ass. Abruptly she stopped turned grabbed my hand and ran my fingertips through the roll-a-dex of her bodies desires. Caribbean dreams of the strokes of my tidal waving rhythm caressing crashing consuming her shores. Volcanic eruptions of her hot Lava'd expulsions racing down my mountains firmness again and again and again. Her excitement told me the custodian had not been this deep in a section of the library ever before. We moved from the romance to the history section and back. It seems as if we had been here before. Her passions desires convulsions seemed all too familiar to me. Her river now and ocean from the deep sea diving pearl grasping sensations of my tongue, her waters sloshed gently and flowed serenely until they came to reside as a pool entrenched in my

goatee. Completely drained, exhausted, satisfied and fulfilled I'd

done all the research I needed. As I walked by her desk on the

way out she slid me her card licked her lips and stated. "Please

come again and use my resources.

Dream Loving

Imagine me breaking you down until you succumb to the feel of my touch, the warmth of my mouth, the chocolate coated breath taking strokes of me. Deep in you, deeply stroking the clock of your passion with both hands, it's only a matter of time until you explode releasing the tones of climax which are a delicacy for my ears to dine upon. Your appetizing lip bitten moans softly whispering sweet nothings in my ear, induced by the sweet something that is the warmth of my mouth on your body. Your sighs harmoniously rising to the ceiling and falling caressing coating my ear lobes with seduction catapulting my arousal to a stage far beyond erection causing me to stroke faster, grind deeper, hit every angle on your compass of satisfaction as I navigate your waters to the shores of orgasm. The screams of your arrival beat the drums of my ears to a tone of "Damn you are all over my spot."

Understand I came to give you exactly what you've been

asking for. A romantic night of bubble bath by candle light and warm oiled massage that leads to your body screaming devour me, and I intend on doing just that. Devour the stimulation of mind, the pleasures of body and the treasures of reaction. With attentive detail watching the reactions of your body my kisses from neck to belly button causing your body temperature to rise, ascending to the heights of arousal. The way your nipples stood erectly in anticipation of my mouths return. Each touch of my fingers along your skin midnight's stroke of sensuality, ten resounding echoes of stimulation talking to your excitement, followed by the eleventh toll of my lips and the final climactic stroke of my tongue. Slowly taking control of your passion, the motion of your hips rise and fall answering its own question of what exactly did I get myself into? The rise of intimacy's seduction riding clouds in the shape of tongue to clit causing the fall of your passions coconut honeyed drops to rain from your lips down to your thighs.

Wait... That's not it. Calm down, catch your breath, and get it together... Big inhale, hold, big exhale, good. Are you good? Are you ready? Come on. Walk with me to a place where only pleasure exists. Our souls intertwined with the comfort of knowing one another intimately, exclusively. Together alone in a world created by the solitude of you and I. molded to the shape of our inner most desires and fantasies. A solitary confinement of MMM that feels so good, I can't believe this is real. Where the only thing that is relative is you and I getting off on us, getting it on to the rhythm of our: Heavy breathing, waist clutching, steady freaking, taste lusting, syncopated, heart beating, knee shaking, starry eyed seeing, thigh trembling, body convulsing, sigh giving, hotly pulsing, hand in hand chest to breast love making. Our souls dance across a marbled floor of happiness moving to the soundtrack of our bodies' erotic encounter between satin sheets. A soundtrack entitled Eroticism. Track one the intro of two souls destined to ride the channels of loves air waves. Track two us becoming acquainted through late night conversation and midnight pillow talk, an a Capella of verbal stimulation. Track three the meeting of minds understanding we need to allow this mid tempo encounter to develop into the slow sultry love ballad that we know we both truly desire. Followed by track's 4-play of touching, caressing and stimulating mind, body and soul. Silhouettes' sliding along one another until they find the perfect position for teasing. Track five a freaky interlude that finds me running shaved ice across your breasts, gently erotically slurping the trail of Malibu Rum from your waist to belly button to nipples down to thighs. Tracks six to nine are a constant loop of us nibbling, slurping, licking, and gulping at one another's pleasures. Track ten the perfection of your walls squeezing convulsing to my strokes. A multi- platinum orgasmic production created by you and I, so tell me Ms. Can you get with that?

Pleasure Smith

Vision me stroking the waters of your excitement molding the very shape of your passions depths with the girth of my instruments long deep pounding strike. The very first strike piercing the sensuous heat of your pond causing your waters to recede momentarily as they are parted by my down stroke while my upstrokes partial withdrawal entices the excitement of your waters as they rise like the morning tide awaiting the return of my hammering injections. The smoldering heat of my pleasure melts away your inhibition and as your desire succumbs to my desire to please you in every way possible our bodies meld into one. Slowly I'll pull away and reposition your ankles around my neck as my tongue introduces himself to lips, hood, clit and inner most desires. The firm grips of your thighs squeezing and constricting around my shoulders only urge my tongue to dive deeper into the compact confides of your pleasure box. The grasp of your palm on the back of my head causes beads of sweat to run down my forehead, pause on my brow and then dive into the recess of your belly button until it becomes filled with the dew of stimulations hard work. Erotically I'll nibble and slurp harder at your excitement letting you know that you can move your hand because there is no reason to guide me, because in all actuality the wetter you get the more I become excited. Tongue's strokes urge you, invite you, beg you, demand that you give in and climax for a second time. Pulling back gazing into your eyes and licking my lips I roll you onto your stomach. Your body cringes from the sheer pleasure of my hard as steel, heavy duty anvil of orgasmic delight entering its realm of seductively moist bliss. Stroke by stroke my repetitive hammering sensations break you down, and the feel of my hammers joy is complimented by the feel of my hand grips on your waist pulling you back to me vigorously. You begin to mumble at the pleasure you're feeling but I assure you that no words are needed. "Don't try to speak just let the freak out and talk to me by bouncing it back to me, wind your hips, as a matter of fact do me like you want to be done. Better yet take that! Here take this and… and take that!" Convinced that you've had enough and sure that your walls have conformed to my girth and how I bend to the left I'll allow my hammering strokes to

orgasmically convulse inside you shaping the pleasure of your

desires.

Loving in Pleasures Sanctuary •LIPS•

Imagine you and I alone in a room filled to capacity, a capacity of sensuality only limited by the imagination. Two beings intertwined by seductions intoxication we become enraptured in the vineyards of curiosity. Let me drink the sun ripened honeyed nectar of your essence. May I be the chocolate Aquarian that draws the waters from the wells of your soul? I stood asphyxiated, outside of time in momentary temporal displacement, frozen, paused by lusts' remote control as he jealously watches me watching you. As you sensually stroke your thighs inner to outer in slow, sultry, stimulating circular motions fingertip to fingertip until they reach the apple bottomed caramel coated firmness of your ass. At which time your palms grope each cheek. I slowly make my way towards watching you repeatedly go from fingertip to palm and back to fingertip. Anxiously anticipating the moment I replace your hands with my lips. Penetrating the aura of your passion with my tongue sliding it along your satin skin like an ice skater carefully twisting, twirling, swirling, engraving eroticism into each breath you take. Our bodies lay in celestial ecstasy aligned perfectly like a solar eclipse.

Six LIPS two tones…the tones of your sighs exhilarating, titillating, filtrating down to my ears, the tones of my slurps suckling upon the essence of you. Our lips engage in soft sensual conversation without a word ever being spoken. Lay there let me enjoy the pleasures of your lips as I step back to gaze upon the beauty of them. A warm refreshing cotton candied dream land in which men fantasize about vacationing to escape reality. To escape the monotonous reoccurring situations of everyday life and reside in the luke warm, lollipop flavors of your lips. We become lip locked in pleasures that seem so unreal that your waters which are usually so calm and steady begin to rise like the early mornings tide. Sloshing back and forth like a childish wave frolicking at play your lips quiver releasing soft subtle murmurs that yearn to express the joy felt by them. As we become tongue tied Tip to Pearl.

Ms. Molasses

I walked in on her, lights off; candles lit Sade "No ordinary Love" playing in the background. The silhouette of her shapely hour glass figure called to me. "The time is right, the time is now, come take time to learn my pleasures." Her eyes closed, head back, back molded perfectly into an arch over two pillows. One hand spreading her lips, the other stroking the pearl of her ocean, I moved closer and sat gently beside her, carefully not to disturb her. I whispered softly in her ear. "Woman you are oh so nasty." She replied, "And you love it." Actually I do I replied. She invited me. "Won't you dine on the delicacies of my passion." How could I deny temptations of chocolate lemonade: the flavors of chocolate so deep, rich and inviting lust, the juices of lemons a bitter taste in my mouth knowing this moment is only temporary and would soon end. The refreshing thirst quenching waters of knowing satisfaction again and again. I ran my tongue from her neck to her hips suckling, slurping gently nibbling an ambrosia created for the most divine moment of ecstasies pleasures. She rolled over onto her stomach sprawled across the sheets and enticed me to insert my circumcised rod of thrusting into her platinum laced diamond cased jewel that she referred to as addiction.

Once More

My body's been craving starving for the feel of your touch. My mind's been wandering back through times portal of passion just to catch a glimpse of you: Eyes closed, lips trembling, fists clinched tightly body glistening perfectly like a flawless diamond under my tongues microscope. My tongue engaged in actions of twirling, twisting from lip to lip slurping from each thigh to clit to thrusting gently into your coca rum intoxication. Preparing you for the initial penetration, gently I slid me in you, and it was as if time stopped, sound paused and sensuality took throne to our souls. Our bodies' became numb from the pleasures of that initial penetration. With long slow deep intense movements I began stroking with conviction. In, out, up down…. I noticed you liked how I curved to the left like a thick candy cane right into your spot. Slowly I stepped back staring at you. Legs still quivering milkshake still avalanching around my mountain as I withdrew. A lake of stimulations labor had formed in the recess of your belly button. You gaze at me. There I stood a well endowed chocolate coated Michael Angelo sculpture. Completely aroused heart racing totally erect, pre-cum anticipating our next encounter I rolled you over onto all fours slipped slid into you and with one hand wrapped around your waist I began stroking your pearl to the rhythm of my strokes. My insertions the booming bass drum my fingers stroking your clit the fast paced circular motion of a hi hat brushed, the erotic expulsions of your juices the perfect accent of a crisp snare. You walls convulsing around me the bouncing bass line of a dance hall calypso's rhythmic pulse. All topped by the soft subtle Sade –Teena Marie melodic harmonies of your sighs. All creating a song that was driving me to a climax I'd never experienced before. There I was lost in the way your ass cheeks rippled, tidal waved from my deep injections of throbbing seduction. When I was brought back to reality by the marshmallow Jacuzzi warmth of your tongue on my manhood. As you slurped me smacked your lips and stated to me, Love you taste like Chocolate Grey Goose. Simply stated intoxicating lustful desire.

Ventilation

She stepped from the shower, body still moist from its encounter with the water and wrapped tightly in a towel. She stepped slowly and made her way to the bed adjusting the towel so that it snugly outlined the curves of her physique. She lay across the bed so that it could get a little air. A gentle breeze blew across her back down her spine over the softness of her ass and down to her toes and back up between her thighs where its draft mixed with the waters of her moisture. Slowly she allowed her hand to travel across her body from breast beyond waist line to the area that she referred to as addiction. Eyes locked on the pages of her favorite book; mind engulfed in the words of a world of erotic pleasure she relaxed into the feel of her fingers caressing her lips with gentle strokes. Arousal raced from the balls of her feet through her thighs into her stomach up her spine and along her arms in the form of a tingling sensation that corresponded with the fondles of her fingers along her pearled switch of excitement. As her strokes became fondles and fondles became the pleasurable motion of insertion and withdrawal complimented by the winding caress of her pearl he walked in the room. Removing his shirt and tie he made his way to the edge of the bed watching her go from lips to pearl and back taking notice of her fingers exact movements and how she liked it stroked. Dropping to his knees he placed his hands on her waist and replaced her fingers motions with those of his tongue. Duplicating the movements of her fingers with his lips and tongue he inserted tongue's tip into her passion as he used his lips to spread hers making sure that his tongue would have unrestricted travels as it caressed her walls in vigorous winding motions. With his tongue spiraling into the depths of seduction he took a firm grasp of her waist and began rocking it gently to the motions of his tongue's darts of in and out, half way in and out, to complete immersion on to the conversion of circular licks and grinding tongues tip across the width of her pearl. Gasping for breath conflicted by asking for less while pleading for more her hands grasped the sheets and her book fell to the floor as his gentle nibbles brought her mind back to a reality of something tangible that was worlds apart from the words which had just occupied it but parallel it's erotic sensations to perfection. His actions mirrored the fictitious detail that sent her mind on an unsequestered romp through an orgasmic dimension of pleasure unknown by most. However his lips diction was a nonverbal nonfiction reality of delight that started her legs twitching and stomach trembling as his mouths slurps ironically sent a cold gust of air across her inner thigh that caused the nectar of her caramel shored lagoon to cascade across his lips. Short of breath and hard to death he pulled back to allow the passion in the air to fill his lungs and once refilled he sprung back into action striving for satisfaction liking her reaction of sigh vending, thigh trembling bliss filled screams so he nibbled on. Sensing that she was ripe for the plucking he rose from his knees and entered her sanctuary of pleasure.

X-Rated

X-Lovers

Reunited by the booming bass in the club although we hadn't seen one another in 3 months what could one dance hurt? One dance turned into two, two into three and three into four…4play of waist twisting, torso grasping, freakish grinding to the steel drum calypso music.

X-stasy

Took over as our hips moved closer in one synonymous rhythm to the classic slow song, while you invited yourself back to my place all the way there my mind racing back to the future reminiscing on the nights of pleasure we've shared and anticipating what was to come.

X-Marked

Your spot: moist, wet, and drenched from the anticipation of me touching you. My tongue honed in on the small of your back, in slow circular winding motions as you arched your back into the perfect position allowing me to slide my tongue from the small of your back to stroking your chocolate coated strawberry walls.

Eagerly I awaited your passion to glaze my tongue and reside in its final resting place of my goatee.

X-Ponentially

The passion grew as I slid me in you although it had been three months it seemed as if it were just yesterday the way your walls conformed to the shape of me. Your clit rising every time I down stroked. As if the goddess of satisfaction hand molded me especially for you, the way I curved to the left directly into your spot. The thickness of me caressing your walls and G Spot each stroke sensually knocking on your back door and the way you gently squeezed and released palpating to my insertions and withdrawal were amazing. Each pulsation became more intense contracting more rapidly until you lost control. Your thighs quivering stomach trembling release of a warm tropical down pour of sensualities nectar.

X-tra Carricular

Was the best way to describe what I woke up to. The feel of sensual relaxation, my body still numbly tingling from the joy of last night's experience: the fresh smell of pancakes, the sight of you in T-shirt and panties. Panties soaked with the essence of seduction, legs overtly spread, and hands caressing thighs to hips to clit. You licking your lips slowly moving to the direction of our eye contact to your panties and enticing me to a breakfast of us.

Desire

Vision us overcoming anticipation by enduring the excitement of anticipation. An anticipation caused by the idea of us enjoying the pleasure of uninhibited moments of satisfaction. Will you walk with me down this path called fulfillment as step by step I guide you through the elation of walls convulsions screaming don't stop? Why would I ever stop slurping, licking, stroking and pleasing you exactly the way that you desire to be pleased? My uncontrollable desire to please you engulfed in learning more of what it is that you enjoy while demonstrating the ability to make your body respond to its touch, its request to undress reticence, renounce hesitation and freely enjoy the moment. Please enjoy the moment in the same manner that I savor every sip of your essences' flavor sliding along my tongue, your fingers caressing the width of my shoulders inviting my desire to dive even deeper into the exhilarating flavors of your taste, the arousing plush texture of your feel; your feel showing its appreciation by the release of climactic nectars sweetly glazed delight. Wont you allow me to be your delight you see there is no need for hopes, dreams or promises because I am the tangible titillation of orgasm personified by your short of breath heartfelt gasps and barely audible sighs. Would you mind if we dive straight in and allowed the contortions of my tongue to become intimate with the movements of your hips, the ardent core of your searing warmth, the candy cream sensations of your arousal. Damn the vibrant convection of your arousal conveyed, relayed through the palpations of your pink ocean of bliss contracting and massaging the dexterity of my tongue. The way your waters rise to my tongues insertions a hospitable current of incalescent honey dew ecstasy and the way your waters ripple around my tongues strokes more than a thrill, causing anxieties eagerness to run rampant while holding hands with let's not wait another moment enticing you to give in to my mouths feel, its pleasure, it subtle demand that you relinquish the keys to exactly what it is that moves you to the tropics of climax.

Neapolitan

She spread her legs inviting the fullness of my stroke, showing an eagerness to see if she could take the complete length of my stroke without its ferocity encouraging her to sprawl, claw, scoot, run away from its deep pounding sensations and I was going to test her will by seeing just how long she'd fight off the desire to do so with long grinds from left to right, hard pummeling strokes from up to down, short quick thrusts from right to left, and slow intent strokes of the tip of my dick across her G-SPOT. I took my chocolate tool of pleasure and brushed it slowly along her lips. Her eyes moved down as she enjoyed the show, begging me to take my chocolate coated thick as peanut butter caramelized in molasses rod of stroking and insert it into the sensation of her warmth. She mumbled "ooh baby take all of that chocolate put it in me, stroke me with it until my waters coat it, no soak it and then let me slurp the flavors of me off of you." However I didn't comply I continued on massaging this chocolate pole along her lips to clit, placing the head in a position so that it rested against her pleasure bordering on penetration causing her clit to remove its hood as her waters rose beyond the edge of her lips capacity and I could feel the erotic pulsing vibration of her pussy yearning for initial penetration resounding from walls, vibrating through lips and echoing through the tip of my dick. Giving in to excitement she pushed her hips forward thrusting me into her moisture. As my chocolate submerged into her pink pond of delight she began to gently nibble on her bottom lip as her eyes closed and her thighs trembled through a quick pleasure induced adjustment. The feel of her pink palace of love was a warming assurance of comforting bliss. Its embrace was the sensual wrap of a Boa Constrictor clothed in Egyptian Cotton sheets fresh out of the drier enticing me to relax and let go yet every time I exhaled it tightened, squeezing me into a pleasure induced coma daring me to find a way to escape, begging me to never leave and coaxing me into residing in its cotton candy fields of arousal forever. I couldn't stay away if I wanted to, not with the way her pink sugared walls were gripping me sensually, grasping me seductively groping me in a manner that whispered to my up stroke "Don't be gone too long because my grip can prolong erections and the sensations of orgasms as long as you come to me, come for me, come back to me so please don't be gone too long." Her pink embered furnace of orgasmic bliss warmed with each down stroke until my chocolate tool of stroking became the fudged wick of stimulation to her waxed pink shea buttered vice of seduction. Soon her waxed pink shea buttered vice of seduction began to melt with each of my long, deep, pummeling strokes and moved to conforming to the shape of my chocolate fudged thickness. I quickened the pace but not to the point of haste because I was thoroughly enjoying the even mixture of her bubble gum pink walls being pulled by the girth of my chocolate and from the stomach shuttering, eye rolling, guttural moans of her reactions so was she. The air tight grips of her pink cotton candy began the increased tempo and ferocity of my chocolate jack hammers down strokes which in turn lead to her body's convulsions as she released the creamy white nectar of orgasm. I leaned over and whispered in her ear "One down two to go" and began to stroke with more intensity until the sounds of tempos smacks bounced off the walls and she released another sample of coconut milk orgasmic bliss, which enticed me to explode and rain candied drops of pleasure, as her pink walls convulsed around my chocolate causing the subtle expulsions of both of our climax to drench the sheets, slide along dick and paint the fixtures of her walls creating the perfect Neapolitan playground of climax.

Stroke

No need to remind me my memory is perfect

I know you like me deep from the left and hard from the back

You enjoy long slow grinds just the way that I work it

And when I hit it doggy style and make the ass go smack

When you're home all alone reminiscing on my... Stroke

Or if we're pressed chest to breast tongue kissing as I... Stroke

Nights when I'm not there you're missing my... Stroke

Your sighs of how you love it complementing my... Stroke

Your moans called for me to intensely go deep

Until pleasures tears caressed your face and you choked up

As the joy of my repetition put you to sleep

The very reason or lack thereof you and your last man broke up

When he's paddling to your shores…Stroke

When she's straddling on all fours…Stroke

When he's traveling from lips to back door…Stroke

When she's babbling and wants more…Stroke

The cause that affects your stomachs convulsion

As your nails dig into the depths of my spine

Making you release your coconut lava hot expulsion

I'm the ultimate pleasure to soul, body and mind

Climactic pleasure has me tempted to…Stroke

Recline into your favorite position as I…Stroke

From the night through the morning with conviction I'll…Stroke

Your fantasy's spot I'll be hitting as I …Stroke

SPECIAL THANKS

Kumasi Lewis: Cover Photo KHL Photography(213)944-4489

Sharaud Moore: Sharaud@SharaudMoore.com

Sequoia Neff Real Estate

Uniquely Sweet Bakery: https://m.facebook.com/UniquelySweet.LA
(310)597-0995

Morris Gamble: https://m.facebook.com/morris.gamble.35

www.ingramcontent.com/pod-product-compliance
Lightning Source LLC
Chambersburg PA
CBHW051645260626
47170CB00004B/1336